# BAD GIRLZ

ALSO BY SHANNON HOLMES

*B-More Careful: A Novel*
*The Game: Short Stories About the Life*

# SHANNON HOLMES

## BAD GIRLZ

**ATRIA** BOOKS

NEW YORK  LONDON  TORONTO  SYDNEY  SINGAPORE

**ATRIA** BOOKS
1230 Avenue of the Americas
New York, NY 10020

ISBN 0-7394-3891-3

**ATRIA** BOOKS is a trademark of Simon & Schuster, Inc.

Manufactured in the United States of America

*To Laila Elise Holmes,*
*for all that you are and all we will ever be.*

*To George Holmes, Jr., I never thought I'd be dedicating*
*a book in ya memory, but Allah knows best. I love you.*
*Not even death could break our bond.*

*To Jules Jackson, Sr.*

*To my family members who recently passed:*
*Cousin Joseph Nublett, Jr.; Aunt Burdell Shuler;*
*Morris "Boo" Smalls; Uncle June Bug; and Uncle Morris.*
*Rest in Peace.*

# A C K N O W L E D G M E N T S

First and foremost, I wish to thank GOD (excuse me fa sounding corny!). Without you, I wouldn't be in the position I'm in. Here I am, a poor lil black boy from da Bronx, armed only wit a GED and street knowledge, and now I'm an author. Wow!!!

Somebody once said to me, "Shannon, I didn't know you could write." I replied, "Me neither!" God, I know you're behind that. Da day I start writing strictly for money (without any moral to the story) is da day I wish for you to take back ya blessing. Till then, ride wit me!!

Next, I would like to thank the Simon & Schuster staff, especially Malaika Adero, Demond Jarrett and Judith Curr. Thanks for believing in my work, allowing me to say it in my way and signing me to a hefty six-figure deal (a deal that has da whole industry buzzing . . . it's the first of its kind for my genre). What's my next deal gonna look like? Just jokin'! I'm just happy to be able to provide fa my family doin' what I luv doin'. How many people can say dat?

Thanks to the Vines Agency, for brokering my deal.

Thanks to my parents, Bob and Elease Holmes. (I'm glad to have made y'all so proud afta all the shame I brought the family name. There's more where this came from.) To my brothers, Bobby (Shon) and Derrick Holmes. To my sisters, Cynthia Martin, Rita and Shonta Holmes. To my nieces, Tenise Cunningham, Negina Holmes (get well soon!), Jeniya Martin, Deja Culpepper

Holmes, Artasia Koon and Ieshia. To my nephews Paul "Ramel," Kasseem "KK," Andre Martin, Dashawn and Donshea Holmes, Scottie Cabrera, Rahsaan Rossberry, Shakeem "Keemie" Smalls, Haseem, and Ramel. To Barbara and Mrs. Lewis. (Ya'll have become like family to me. Love ya.)

To my Aunt Juanita Holmes (Savannah, GA) and the rest of my extended family in Macon and Atlanta. Thanks for your support. To Philly Lewis and her daughter Lauren. Cousins Latisha Moore, Joanna Moore, Amar Moore. (Keep doing whatcha doing! You got a good heart. God is going to bless you.) To my family on lock: Jamel Smalls, Saeed Kaide, Tuheed "Tony" Mitchell and Dahoo Allen a.k.a. Ricky Schuler (hold ya head). Vicky Stringer (*Let That Be the Reason*), thanks for reaching out to me and extending your friendship through thick and thin. There was never a rivalry between us. Though certain people put us at odds, we saw through that.

In the immortal words of Tupac "You ain't neva hada friend like me." My n**** Anthony Whyte (*Ghetto Girls*). Dogz, you too have reached out to me and we've become close. It goes beyond this book thing. I want fa you what I want fa myself: success. One luv!

Darren Coleman (*Before I Let Go*), me and you met unda unusual circumstances. I reached out to you and gave some advice, which you wisely heeded. Since that day we've become close (you lookin' out fa me and vice versa). As I go through these literary doors before you, I'll continue to tell you what's on the other side. I won't keep nuttin' secret. Nicky Turner (*A Hustler's Wife*), my li'l sis. Yo, I wish you all the best in da world. I once told you that I wanna give anybody that's rollin' wit me the best advice I can give em, regardless of what it is. (Neva let it be said that Shannon Holmes came between you and some money. Neva dat!) Just be patient. Everything you want will be in ya grasp. Just continue writing fa da love and the rest will follow. I Love you gurl! I swear I do! Ha! Ha!

Kwan (Gangsta) You are clearly not the same person I met last year. Somebody has gotten in ya ear. And they probably ain't in da industry. I thought you would be the Robin ta my Batman. But it wuzn't ta be. Clearly you had other plans, ulterior motives. You have taught me to "B-more careful" of whom I let in my circle. I coulda pulled ya coat ta so many things, but. . . . Nevermind. . . . You got da game all figured out!

Much love to Travis Hunter (*Heart of Men*), Brenda Thomas (*Threesome*), Oscar (at *Our Black Heritage* on 135th Street), Lacey (*Love, Life & Loneliness*), *Hue-Man* books (125th Street), Ms. Villarosa and Mrs. Ewing. To Monique Patterson (St. Martin's Press), Zane (Nice meeting you. You got the blueprint I'm tryin' ta follow. You go gurl!).

Much love to Carol and Brenda (*C&B Distribution*). Ya'll my peeps! I will always keep it real. To *Bronx Book Palace, Hermena*, my street team *Hawkins "Hawky" Books & CD's* (125th Street)—a lot of love for ya'll. Mr. Reid (*Seller Books* in Jamaica Queens), we gonna do big things. Much love to Diana (*Books Plus* in Brooklyn), Nicky (the bartender at *Harry's Triangle*), Goody, Unique (a.k.a Rhonda) and Destiny (good looking). Shout-out to *Harry's Triangle* staff.

I wrote in my last book, "If I forgot ya name, charge it to my head, not my heart." But obviously y'all didn't hear me. Some of y'all really hurt me to my heart wit ya pettiness. Can y'all just be happy fa me? Somebody finally made it off the block, legally. Those who were there know! This may be the last time I ever do this.

Thanks to da Block: Jfish Avenue and Boston Road. Thanks to Junie (a.k.a. Black Caesar), Franklin "Junior" Greenway, Ronald "Oriental" Bryant (Sit tight my n*****—I'm 'bout ta do us!).

Mark Sandy; Curly "Mo-Dollar" Bennet (come home soon); Dave Cook (I kept my word!); Richie Tee (How could I forget you?); Soldier; Clarkie; Tank; Universal; Jerry "Sha" Brisbane and Trevor "Skatts" Sing; Lamont "Cheese" Harris; Michael "Knott" Palmer; Rich-Mo; Lil Danny; Floyd Murray; Half Pint a.k.a. Jules Jackson, Jr.; Jerome Miller (aka Basic); Georgie "G" Edenwald; Pretty Boy Floyd; Simon; Jip; Juice; DJ Stan Strong. My homegirls Roslyn "Poopie" Bryant, Alicia "Butter" Mayes, Monique and Tracy Adams, Vicky Vail a.k.a. Maria, Debbie, Talisa, LeLe, Nahleen Smalls, Lauren Stevens, Ms. Linda Johnson (Canarsie, Brooklyn), Sharisse (get well soon!), Shanora Sherri Middleton. Thanks to 220th St. Lorenzo "THE L" Ellis (Dat's my Boy!), Eric White, the Jackson Family (thank you for embracing me from day one!). To Diana (Smith Cairns Ford), thanks for the sweetheart deal. Kevin Jackson (my trusty assistant), Shamika Jackson (will you???? . . . figure out da rest). B-more Homies: Thomas Long, Robert Wise (Balitmore's finest), Rich, Shamus and Chris Robertson, Chet Parjardo (*Pajardo Wear*), Boosty, Sweets, Gail and Rasheed.

# BAD GIRLZ

THERE IS AN AREA IN NORTH PHILADELPHIA, called the Badlands. It's one of the toughest communities not only in Philly, but in the nation. For decades now the area has been plagued by poverty. This predominantly Hispanic section of town is polluted with crime, guns and drugs. Heroin reigns supreme here; it is the number-one drug of choice. Dealers, fiends and junkies—of all races, from all walks of life—come here from far and wide to cop drugs.

Anywhere you looked in the Badlands, you could see the living dead, men and women so severely addicted to drugs that they are slowly dying. And they know it. Here it is commonplace to see a corpse, as well as syringes and other kinds of drug paraphernalia, lying in the gutter. The Badlands is a place that urban renewal and empowerment zones forgot. The decrepit row houses and rodent-infested tenement buildings that line the blocks are evidence of the fact. Here murder and mayhem are the law of the land.

Pain and suffering are a natural way of life for people in this environment. They are suffocated by negativity and often have no alternative but to engage in destructive behavior. Some buy and sell dreams by selling or using drugs. This is their way to escape a grimy reality. Some sell no less than their souls.

Nestled in with the Hispanic families on 9th and Indiana lived a black family. Something took place in their household that would change a young girl's life forever.

# 1

"C'MERE, TONYA!" her mother yelled, as she passed her coming out of the bathroom. The woman's eyes focused like laser beams on her daughter's neck. Tonya pulled up her shirt collar in response, desperate in her attempt to hide the focus of her mother's attention.

Veronica Morris had forewarned her daughter time and time again about being fast with boys. "Stay away from them. Keep your legs closed. I'm not trying to be a grandmother yet," she repeated. But like any single mother raising a teenaged daughter, she was overwhelmed. Ms. Morris was as strict with Tonya as she could be. She made no concessions. Tonya was seventeen years old, and still not allowed to have a boyfriend, to date boys or even have them call the house. She was a typical teenager though; she found a way to do the normal things that young people do for fun despite her mom. Tonya had always managed to hide any disobedient act from her mother. That is, until now.

Veronica grabbed Tonya by the shirt collar and snatched her back into the bathroom to examine her in the light.

"What the hell is this?" she asked, touching the discolorations along the right side of her daughter's neck.

"Nuttin! . . . I . . . I . . . I was fightin'," Tonya stuttered.

"These ain't no damn bruises or scratches," her mother said. "You think I'm stupid? Huh? Huh? . . ." Her head jerked and she began viciously slapping her daughter in the face.

"You little hussy! You think I don't know passion marks when I see 'em?" She continued slapping her.

"But Mommy, I didn't do nuttin . . ." Tonya cried.

Veronica Morris was a heavyset woman, who was once endowed with a lovely figure, to match her face. But Father Time and neglect had conspired to rob her of her beauty. Her once shapely butt, thighs and hips were sagging under the weight of cellulite. The excess weight that she carried made her heavy-handed; she hit like a man. Tonya was dizzy from the punches against her body.

The mother beat her daughter like she was a stranger, hurling her against the bathroom walls, knocking down shelves and toiletries. She flung the girl to the hard floor and pounded on her back.

"You come home pregnant, heifer, so help me God, I'ma stomp it outta you!" she promised.

Tonya curled up into a fetal position, and wondered what she had done to deserve a beating like this. She let a boy pet and kiss her. And now she was getting the beating of her life.

Veronica was immune to her daughter's pleas and cries. She broke a wooden toilet plunger over the girl's back. She wanted to teach her a lesson, one she would not soon forget.

Veronica knew that there was no better time than the present to be a woman, especially a minority woman. The window of opportunity was wider than ever. She wanted Tonya to avoid the mistakes she herself had made. She became a teenaged mother and was robbed of her once promising future. She didn't want her daughter to follow in her footsteps.

The last thing she wanted was for Tonya to succumb to the soft touch, the careless whisper, the lies and deceit of a boy, who had vowed they would be together forever, only to abandon her in her time of need. No, she longed for Tonya to go to college, graduate, get married, make it out of the ghetto, and not get stuck in some menial job, living paycheck to paycheck. After Tonya's father left Veronica, she ate. Food became her friend. Her weight then ballooned to outrageous proportions, making her unattractive to most of the men around her, except for Pete. He happily accepted her and was willing to take care of her child too. Pete loved big women, even though he was 125 pounds, soaking wet.

Veronica could not look at Tonya, much less strike her, without being reminded of her daughter's no-good father, Raymond. Tonya looked just like him. The resemblance caused Veronica to feel, again, and again, the pain of a broken heart, the sting of rejection, and the words of a broken promise.

She had a live-in boyfriend but not even her relationship with him could heal the wound. Pete woke up when he heard all the commotion. Partially clothed, he rushed into the bathroom.

"That's enough, Veronica!" he said, as he bear-hugged her and dragged her out the bathroom. "You gonna kill that po' girl."

"Lemme go!" she pleaded. "And I will kill that hot heifer!"

When her mother was safely out of the room, a hysterical Tonya got up off the floor and looked into the mirror. She had a puffy right eye, a split lip and a bloody nose.

"I didn't even do nuttin'," she sobbed, and tried to clean herself up.

Tonya passed her mother in the small apartment hallway while heading to her room, and flinched. Veronica had almost forgotten that she would be due to show up for work. Shortly, she was on her way out to get to her job as a home attendant.

"Don't take ya hot ass ta school taday!" Veronica ordered.

More than anything she was scared some nosy school official would question her daughter about her bumps and bruises. She didn't want to risk arrest on child abuse charges or her daughter being removed from her home by some child welfare agency. "I ain't finished wit you, Ms. Thang." That said as she wobbled out the door, off to another hard day of work.

Tonya went to her room, closed her bedroom door, flopped down on the bed and cried some more. She replayed the beating in her mind over and over again. After about an hour or so, there was a knock on her door. It was Pete with a glass of Kool-Aid in his hand.

"Tonya, you alright?" he asked, while he ran his eyes all over her body. Over the years, Pete had earnestly watched as Tonya's body began to fill out. As she was growing up, he would sneak a feel on her young body, under the pretense of horseplay. Seemingly overnight she had arrived at womanhood. The Morris family and close friends had often wondered what Veronica Morris saw in Pete. Other than the SSI disability check he received every month. He was twenty years her senior, and an alcoholic. But love is blind and he had caught Veronica at a vulnerable time in her life. She had just given birth to her only child, Tonya.

"Yeah, I'm okay," Tonya mumbled, sitting back down on her bed.

"You know ya mother didn't mean to do you like that. You know how crazy she gets 'bout you and dem boys."

"Look at my face!" she screamed. "She ain't have to go dat far. She coulda talked ta me. Shoot, she ain't no angel, her damn self."

Tonya loved that she could vent all her pent-up frustrations about her mother to Pete, and not have to worry about him repeating her comments. Over the years, he won her trust and became a valued confidant. At times he even acted as a go-between, squashing beefs they had. . . .

"Tonya, you know ya mother only wants the best for you. She

just goes about things wrong sometimes. But that's still ya mother and she loves you."

"Loves me? If she loves me, she sure gotta funny way of showin it. She beat me worse than a dog."

Pete sighed. "I know how you feel. Things did get a little outta hand. But y'all will get through this. Y'all always do. Here, drink this."

"I don't know 'bout dis time. Dis time it's different," Tonya informed him. "She ain't neva beat me like that. I'll neva forget it for as long as I live."

"Don't worry, you will. Just give it some time."

Tonya was thirsty and gulped the drink down in a hurry. Pete leaned up against her dresser and dug into his front pocket. He pulled out a hand-rolled cigarette.

Aside from being a chronic drunk, Pete was a weed smoker, especially when his woman wasn't around. He and Tonya had secretly shared a few joints together on several occasions. Tonya thought that was so cool of him.

"Here," he said, extending his hand. "you light it up. You had a rough day already."

Tonya took the joint and lighter, and without even thinking twice proceeded to do as she was told. She was about to receive a welcomed escape.

Unbeknownst to Tonya, this was not marijuana. This was PCP, angel dust, a hallucinogenic drug that sometimes renders the user dangerous or helpless. A novice weed smoker, she never noticed the strong difference in smell. Maybe she was too mad or distracted to question it. She just wanted to get high. So she inhaled the fumes.

"Hun," she said, handing the joint back to Pete.

"Naw," he responded. "You go 'head and finish it up."

"Okay, but you don't know what you missin'. This weed is pretty good."

Pete did know what he was missing. PCP could sometimes be a terrible high for first-time users. He declined her offer. He wanted to keep his mind right while he did what he planned to do.

The drug took effect. In mid-sentence Tonya's speech became slurred. She visibly began to move slowly, almost robotic. The joint fell out her hands and landed on the floor, as she fell back on the bed. She began seeing spots on the wall.

Pete picked the joint up from the floor and put it in an ashtray. He began stroking himself through his jeans. It didn't take long for his manhood to respond. Looking at Tonya sprawled out across the bed did the trick. The black stretch pants she wore hugged every crevice of her lower body. They were so tight on her thigh and hip area, it seemed like she was about to bust out of them. Tonya's above-average breasts pushed her bra to the limit. His long black rod reached maximum size, bulging out of his pants. She was a fine young thing, the kind that was always out of Pete's reach, even in his youth. He longed for this day when he could act on the sexual fantasies that he had for Tonya.

He undressed, then began to undress her. Tearing at her shirt and bra, he freed her breasts. Then he yanked her stretch pants over her wide hips. When that was done he climbed on top of her, kissing and caressing Tonya, like this was consensual sex and he was making love to her. He stuck his alcohol-laced tongue in her mouth, stealing a one-sided French kiss. Then he slowly ran his tongue all over her copper-toned body, leaving a trail of saliva, from her breasts down. Continuing past her pubic hairs, he reached her vagina. Once there he began rapidly flicking his tongue in and out, lapping up her juices. He made her wet, preparing her for penetration. Tonya didn't respond because she couldn't under the influence of the angel dust. He took his time. He knew that Tonya's mom wouldn't be home anytime soon. Rock hard, he was now ready to enter her. Spreading her thick thighs apart, Pete inserted the head of his penis into her warm vagina, slowly working in a little of his large manhood at a time. Tonya was so tight, he thought he had died and gone to heaven. Bit by bit, he crammed the rest of himself inside her. She was a virgin. A thin coat of blood formed on his uncircumcised penis. He had popped her cherry. If she had been sober, she would have been in pain. But as it was, she was just a prisoner, unable to fend off a predator.

Sweat rolled off his body as he pounded away at her vagina. In his twisted mind, he felt like he was owed this—for all the years he supported her, all the years her mother robbed him of his checks. Pete humped himself into a frenzy. The head of his penis began to swell, he was about to explode. Pulling out in the nick of time, he shot cum all over the girl's stomach and chest. Still Tonya didn't even move. Drained, he sat on the edge of the bed, hyper-ventilating.

Resting in between, Pete violated her over and over for hours. He placed Tonya in all kinds of positions. He even sodomized her. He lived out his wildest fantasies on her and she was power-less to stop him.

When Pete was done, he gently washed Tonya up and put clothes on her. Then he tucked her in bed, as if she were sleeping. He then went to gather up his clothes and left the apartment.

Tonya drifted into sleep. This was a good thing. She was able to sleep off the ill effects of the angel dust. Veronica Morris en-tered the house and went straight to her daughter's room. All throughout her work shift she thought about Tonya and what she had done to her. She knew she had gone off the deep end. Having had a change of heart, her intention was to apologize for her out-rageous behavior. Something stopped her when she entered her daughter's room. She smelled the stench of sex in the air. She smelled the strong body odor of her man, Pete, as well. Further, she looked at the covers on Tonya's bed and noticed the blood and cum stains. The rage that she'd let go of returned in a flash. She paced back and forth. Then she went over to her daughter's TV, took the extension cord from it, and began to beat Tonya awake.

"Aaahh! What you doin'?" Tonya screamed.

"Bitch, I should be askin' you that question. Who was you fuckin' up in *my house? Huh?*"

Tonya rolled off the bed, ducking and dodging her mother. She tried to shake off the drowsiness. Her legs were like rubber. She couldn't get away from her mother fast enough. She began to feel sharp pains coming from her anus and vagina. What had happened to her? she thought. But she was more worried about avoiding the vicious stings from the extension cord.

"You li'l tramp!" her mother hollered. "You was in here seducing my man? Huh?"

"I don't know what you're talkin' 'bout," Tonya cried. "Why are you doin' this ta me? Where is your man?" she shouted.

Suddenly she stopped whipping her daughter. It was as if something clicked in her head. She left the room to look for Pete.

Tonya curled up on the floor in the corner of her room, crying, burning up from the licks inflicted upon her inside and out. She strained her brain trying to recall what had happened to her over the last few hours. Her mind was flooded with images of her mother and Pete, treating her like a dog.

Storming back into the room, her mother said, "Go get yaself cleaned up. We goin' to da hospital." The nurses and doctors drilled the woman and her daughter with questions they wouldn't and couldn't answer.

They administered a rape kit, though Veronica tried to deny that a rape could have occurred. She was angrier than ever, but at Tonya. She wanted to believe that her daughter brought this on herself and her household. She also wondered, Where the hell was Pete?

Veronica checked Tonya out of the hospital, but it took a whole lot of talking to convince the doctors that she was actually going to the police. Veronica and Tonya spent the following days avoiding each other as much as they could. Each stayed behind the closed door of their bedrooms or the bathroom. Tonya longed for her mother to say something or to touch her. Veronica's ego wouldn't allow her to be a mother and do what she could to make things right for her child.

Months later, Tonya came home from school and thought her home had been burglarized. The apartment was empty. It wasn't until she saw that everything was gone except her clothes that it occurred to her that her mother had moved out. There was no note, no forwarding address left for Tonya. She was on her own.

TONYA WOULD HAVE FIRST GONE to her grandmother but she had died. So she bounced around from family member to family member for months, looking for a stable home. She found no takers. Her mother had dragged her name through the mud, ruining the girl's reputation with their family. She told the story of how her household was broken and made Tonya the villain.

Tonya's aunts and female cousins saw her as a threat to their own happy homes and relationships. To them, she was just another hot freak. If she did it with her own mother's man, then she'd do it to anybody's, they reasoned. In the absence of her maternal grandmother, there was no one left to give any motherly guidance and love.

Her uncles and male cousins became predators, trying to get in her pants every chance they got. They wanted to believe the rumors about her being a freak. They even propositioned her with money.

Tonya rode the L train back and forth, as much as she could. Otherwise, she would catch a few z's at the Greyhound bus station, until she was run out of there. Wherever she could get some shut-eye, in peace, she laid her head. She ate at soup kitchens with total strangers. Then she began to trade food and shelter for sexual favors.

The neighborhood boys began passing her around, sneaking Tonya into their bedrooms late at night, feeding her, having sex with her, and getting rid of her by morning. Having sex brought back the rape and her mother's sudden departure every time she did it. Pete and her mother took her innocence, shattered her heart and threw her away.

"TONYA, DANCE FA ME," Todd said as he sat back on the bed.

She slowly danced naked to some imaginary rhythm that only she could hear, doused by the red light.

"I don't know if anybody ever told you this," he commented, "but you should be a stripper. I swear on everythang I love, you'd get paid! Tonya, you got one of the tightest bodies I've ever seen."

She moved toward him, continuing to dance. She bent over and brushed her breasts across his face. Playfully, he licked at them. He enjoyed being teased; he enjoyed every minute of her show. She was a bit more relaxed with him than she normally was. Out of all the dudes she slept with, Todd treated her best.

"Seriously, you should think about strippin'. I mean it beats doin' what cha doin'. You know." He felt bad about using her the way he did. It wasn't right and he knew it. But rather than say so, he'd at least try to help her out. "Listen, I gotta cousin named Katrina from West Philly who dances. I'll introduce you to her. And she can definitely plug you in."

She wasn't sure whether this was good news or not but she said "Aiight." Just to shut him up.

"C'mere, girl," he whispered. "Gimme soma that thang."

They fucked themselves to sleep. Early the next morning, Todd awoke and gave his cousin a call. Since they were close like that, she immediately came over. Tonya woke up hearing their loud conversation in the kitchen.

". . . You was right, she is pretty. But . . . damn, how old is she? Ain't no older chick gonna let you young niggas run up in her like that. So she gotta be unda age," Katrina said.

"She almost eighteen," he replied. "But she ain't silly-actin' or young-minded. Shorty just fucked up in da game right now. Dat's all."

Katrina laughed, "Nigga, what you runnin' a fuckin' group home here? I didn't know you cared. Whatever happened to all that Snoop Dogg shit, Bitches ain't shit but hos and tricks. Remember? What you getting soft on me? . . . Go wake her up. Let's see what she tryin' ta do. Hope you ain't have me come out here fa nuttin'."

Todd went to his room and gently shook Tonya awake. She pretended to be fast asleep.

"Huh?" she softly moaned.

"Git up! My cousin's here and she wanna meet you. Now!" he announced.

Tonya climbed out of his warm bed and slipped on a pair of his basketball shorts and a plain white tank top. Following Todd into the kitchen, unsure of what to expect, she was somewhat awestruck by this gorgeous light-skinned girl with long black hair and cold catlike gray eyes.

"How you doin'?" Katrina warmly greeted her. "I'm Katrina, but I dance under the name Kat. My cousin here tells me he thinks you got da goods to be a stripper? Do you wanna dance? . . . I wanna hear it from you? . . . And why?"

Tonya didn't know where to begin or what to say. When she was initially approached with the idea of stripping she thought it was a joke. She only agreed to it to silence Todd. She never thought that he would actually call his cousin. She couldn't believe that he actually took her seriously. But he did. So here Tonya was, on the spot, face-to-face with Kat.

"Yeah, ya cousin told you right," she bashfully admitted. "I wanna strip."

"Girlfriend, you gots to speak a li'l louder than that," Kat said, as she took a good look at her body. Tonya was stacked. She definitely had that in her favor. There was no question about it, she could be a stripper on looks alone. But it took more than that, it took desperation, desire. "Yo, Todd, excuse yaself while us girls talk."

Excusing himself, Todd went back to his room and closed the door.

"Have a seat," Kat told her. "Relax, we 'bout to have a serious talk. Now, what's da deal?"

Tonya sat down at the small kitchen table, directly across from her, and looked her in the eye. She automatically felt something real about Kat, something sincere. Whether this vibe was real or imagined, she didn't know. All she knew was she was at ease around this stranger.

Kat reiterated, with a stern look on her face, "So you 'really' wanna strip, huh?"

"Yeah!" Tonya spoke up.

"Are you positive you wanna do this?" Kat asked again, questioning her motives. "You gotta have confidence to strip. You can't have any hang-ups about ya body. Can't be no shame in ya game. This definitely ain't fa everybody. . . ."

Telling her no, she couldn't or wouldn't was a luxury Tonya didn't have. It wasn't as if she even knew where her next meal was coming from or where she would lay her head. She straddled an imaginary fence, caught between what she knew was wrong and what she had to do. Somewhere in the middle of the two, lay reality—her fate.

"I'm sure I wanna do it," she stated firmly. "I got to. I take care of myself. My family don't fuck with me. It's a long story."

"Well," Kat said. "I got a minute or two. What's up?"

"See, what happened was, my mother's boyfriend gave me a joint of weed. Only it wasn't weed, it was dust. Before I knew what was goin' on, he raped me. And after dat, things with my moms been goin' from bad to worse."

Tonya went on. She told Kat everything while tears trickled down her cheeks. This was the first she'd talked about her situation. Her family hadn't even wanted to listen. Kat was blown away. For all that she had seen and done, she couldn't picture any mother turning against her own daughter like that. Yeah, she thought, I'll take Tonya under my wing.

"Go get ya things," Kat commanded her. "You comin' ta live wit me and my girlfriend, Goldie. She's cool, you'll dig her."

Just like that Kat rescued Tonya off the streets. She was about to show the young girl a hustle, one that wouldn't just feed her for a day, but possibly a lifetime. If she played her cards right.

Tonya's body had been a burden her entire young life, attracting lots of unwanted attention from boys and men alike. But it was about to turn out to be her greatest asset. She was entering a world where men would again only be interested in her body, but at least they would pay good money to see her, and maybe not touch her.

# 2

Tonya was lost in her thoughts staring out the passenger-side window of Kat's white Cadillac Escalade truck. As the music played, she wondered where they were headed. She didn't bother to ask out loud and Kat hadn't said. Tonya was scared and excited at the same time. Scared, because she didn't know what her future held. Excited, because it had to be better than the present.

When guys pulled up alongside Kat's vehicle at a red light, they were shocked to see a woman pushing it. This is a status ride signaling the owner's arrival into the big time. Tonya wondered how could Kat afford it? Was the stripping game that good? She hoped that one day she would be able to get a fly whip like this too.

The truck was Kat's pride and joy. She had it decked out with all the latest accessories, two seven-inch TV monitors mounted in the headrests, one in the visor. And a big fifteen-inch TV that dropped down from the ceiling. The vehicle was also loaded with a PlayStation 2 video game system, a DVD player, twelve-disc CD changer and a hanging stereo system. To top that all off, she sat on twenty-four-inch chrome Ludacris rims.

Pulling up on 82nd and Lindbergh Avenue, Kat guided the big truck to the curb and parked. They exited the car and, with the press of a button, Kat unlocked the rear door so Tonya could retrieve her things.

Grabbing two duffel bags, Tonya closed the rear door and proceeded to follow Kat. While they walked toward a pretty beige-paneled, detached home, Kat reached over her shoulder, pointing the key car alarm in her vehicle's direction, activating the Viper alarm system. The headlights blinked and the alarm chirped.

They moved past the freshly painted white wooden gate, up a short flight of stairs to the porch. As Kat fiddled through her key ring to unlock the door, Tonya scanned the neighborhood. There was a notable absence of drug dealers on the street. She had grown accustomed to them being a permanent part of the land-scape, at least in her own neighborhood. This alone let her know that she was now in an upscale neighborhood.

Kate unlocked the door and they both stepped through the threshold. "Listen," Kat said. She stopped in the hallway. "I don't allow no shoes or sneakers on in my house beyond this point. I got wall-to-wall carpeting. Na'mean?"

"I understand," Tonya replied and slipped off her shoes.

"Thanks," Kat said. "Gotta keep my shit intact. Niggas will fuck ya shit up!"

Carpet was like a foreign substance to Tonya. At home all they ever walked on was bathroom tile and wooden floorboards. She enjoyed the cozy feel of it against the soles of her feet. Her toes sunk into it as she followed Kat down the hall.

Before either of them could get any further, they heard "Mommy!"

"Hey, li'l man!" Kat greeted her son Eric with open arms. They embraced, kissing each other numerous times.

Tonya could see the love and affection that these two shared. The little boy looked well taken care of. He was dressed in blue Sean John jeans with a matching shirt and dark blue Timberland field boots. Everything he had on was new.

The boy's father was incarcerated in Leavenworth Federal Penitentiary and, by giving him everything, Kat was trying to make up for the absence. Eric Sr., had participated in a botched bank robbery that left two armed guards dead. He received a sentence of forever and a day. She exchanged time for money and divided her maternal duties between her mother, an ex-stripper, and her older sister, Jackie, also an ex-stripper, who was now married and a born-again Christian.

"Aiight, li'l man, it's time to get down. You gettin' heavy now," she told him. "Pretty soon you gonna be carrying me."

Her son smiled and wiggled out of her arms and onto the floor.

"Katrina? Is that you?" Jackie called out from the living room.

"Who da hell else could it be?" Kat answered with an attitude. If it was one thing she hated more than stupid people, it was stupid questions.

"Well, why you gotta curse? Especially on the Lord's day. Show some respect," she said.

"Look, dis is *my house!* I cursed 'cause I felt like it," Kat exclaimed.

As they entered the living room, Jackie exclaimed, "Anyway, it's about time you came home. You only a day late, what happened to Saturday?"

Tonya looked around at the living room furnishings in amazement. Big screen TV, massive stereo with surround sound, beige Italian leather living room set, mirrored wall, and a bearskin rug.

"Jackie, Pleeezze! Not now!" Kat replied, sitting on the couch with her son in her lap. "If I wanna hear a sermon I'll go ta church my damn self," Kat replied.

"You just oughta," her sister said.

She fired back, "Nuttin' dat you ain't neva done. Don't get it twisted. Ms. Holier than thou."

"I was ignorant. But that was then, this is now. I've got the Lord in my life. My savior is Jesus Christ . . ." Jackie stated, before changing the subject. ". . . Who's this?" she said, looking in Tonya's direction.

"If you stop preaching for a minute I can introduce you," Kat cracked. "That's my people, Tonya. Tonya, dat's my big mouth sister, Jackie."

The two women exchanged greetings and good looks at each other. Kat offered Tonya a seat and something to drink while Kat went to the kitchen to pour a glass of juice.

"Tonya? . . . You look mighty young. How old iz you, girl?" Jackie asked.

Before Tonya could even respond, Kat intervened. "Don't answer her. She ain't nobody. A nosy nobody at that."

"Katrina, you thirty-one years old and still hangin' wit kids," Jackie said as she cut a look at her sister. "And leadin' them astray straight to the hell fire."

Jackie was famous for bringing up Kat's age, but she was forever doing that and Kat hated it. Kat thought she was forever young. She didn't look a day over twenty-one—she definitely didn't feel it.

"Eric, go in Mommy's room, grown folks are talkin'," she told her son. When he was out of earshot she went off. "Listen here, Jackie, I'm 'bout tired of ya shit! Take ya save the world crusade to da nearest corner in North Philly. Them gangsta-ass niggas need you over there more than I do. 'Cause right now, I ain't feelin' you at all."

"But Katrina," Jackie pleaded, toning it down. "She's just a baby. Please don't take her to that club. That's not cool." If anybody in the world knew Kat, it was her sister Jackie. She knew how Kat got down and she knew what her sister was thinking, probably before she did. She figured that her sister was probably helping this young girl out, but she also figured that Kat had ulterior motives as well. Kat hadn't changed a bit over the years. If anything, she got worse.

"Knock it da fuck off! Okay? You was once a stripper too," Kat growled. "Wasn't nuttin' wrong wit it when you did it. So what's wrong wit it now? Just like you chose not to do it anymore. Somebody else is gonna choose to do it . . . My girl Tonya got problems. It's that serious . . ."

Kat was a risk-taker by nature. Win, lose or draw, she was willing to deal with the consequences of whatever, come what may. And although she was the baby of the family, she was her own woman. Nobody could tell her anything. Stripping was her life. She never had to condition herself to enjoy it, she took to it naturally. Lost in the sauce, she was content with being right where she was. In the mix of all the action.

". . . Tonya got drama. She done lived the life of a forty-year-old woman," Kat said to her sister. "Ain't no right in that. So don't gimme no lectures about right and wrong, good vs. evil. Only God can judge me. The girl need money fast. Ain't nobody lookin' out fa her. I'ma show her how to take care of herself."

"How? By strippin'?" Jackie said. "There's other ways to help her, you know? That's if you really care? If you really wanna help? Katrina, don't turn her on to the strip game. Don't turn her on to nuttin' bad. You don't want that on ya conscience or in the book of deeds when you go meet ya maker. If anything, you should be tryin' to dissuade her from that life. What if you had a daughter? Would you want someone showin' ya child somethin' so negative?"

Ever since Jackie's girlfriend, Candy, got killed some years ago by some obsessed trick she was dating, she decided to do all she could to discourage anyone from stripping and tricking. Jackie took her friend's fate as a sign from God. He was telling her to get the hell out the strip club scene. So she turned over a new leaf and got baptized. In her heart she knew it could have been her in a coffin, at the rate she was going.

"Jackie, you know what?" Kat stated angrily. "It's time fa you to roll out. You fuckin' up my whole vibe early in the morning. I ain't got time fa dis. I ain't arguin' wit you. You don't like what I do? Fine, keep it movin'! Stay da fuck away from me and outta my business . . ."

In the midst of this heated debate, Tonya stood dumbfounded. She was the topic of conversation, yet she was powerless to stop it. This was bigger than her.

"From now on, you can come get ya son yaself from Mommy's house," Jackie spat as she gathered herself and prepared to leave. But before she did, she turned to young Tonya and said, "Keep ya dignity! If you don't stand for somethin', you'll fall fa anything. I'll pray for you too. 'Cause only God knows what you're about to get yaself into . . ."

"Yeah, tell ya story walkin'," Kat said sarcastically. "And tell Ma I'll drop Eric off later. Bye!" As soon as Jackie left, she continued, "Don't pay dat bitch no mind. Don't let her scare you or spook you. Do it fa you! 'Cause ain't nobody gonna do it fa you. Na'mean?"

Unexpectedly, Kat's other houseguest, Gloria Cruz, aka Goldie, came strolling into the house. She was fresh off an overnight date.

"Hey, Hey, Hey, Hey!" she happily exclaimed, mimicking a character off an old TV show. "Yo, Kat, what's up wit ya sister? She just walked by me witout sayin' a word. She looked madder than a motherfucka. What you do to her?"

Gloria was a short pint-sized cutie. A Puerto Rican sex kitten, with bubble-shaped brown eyes, long straight black hair that flowed down her back, and a body that begged to be touched. She and Kat had met some years back under unusual circumstances. And just like Kat was doing for Tonya, rescuing her off the streets, she had done the same for Goldie. She even stuck up for Goldie, on several occasions, protecting her from extortion attempts and unwanted sexual advances at the club. But they shared something much deeper than a friendship, they shared a secret.

"Fuck her!" Kat sighed. "Long story."

"Oh, she trippin' again," Goldie commented. "Quotin' scriptures and shit."

"Yep!" Kat replied. "You know how she gets. Anyway . . . Goldie, dis is Tonya, our new roommate."

"Hey, Tonya," Goldie said, taking right to her. "Girl, grab a seat. You ain't gonna hold up da walls all morning? Is you?"

Tonya smiled and sat down. She still was unsure of what to say next. After a short awkward silence, Goldie spoke. "What, da cat got ya tongue? You can talk, right?"

"Huh?" Tonya responded.

"If you can say huh, you heard," Goldie playfully said. "Girl, talk up. No need to be shy. You around fam. We all in da same gang here."

Tonya grinned at her.

"Listen, Tonya," Goldie stated, "The first thing we have to do is change ya name. You can't be lettin' niggas know ya government like that. That ain't cool. So I suggest we change ya handle now, before anybody gets use to callin' you by ya real name. Kat, any suggestions?"

"Yeah. Bein' dat she's young, how 'bout Baby Girl?" she said.

"Bitch, you been watchin' too much *Good Times*," Goldie joked. "Plus dat's da name of dat dirty bitch outta North Philly you can't stand."

"You right. So, naw, dat won't work," she agreed. "How 'bout Brown Sugar? After all, she is brown-skinned and I always like that record by DeAngelo."

"Naw, you can't get dat off either. We need to be a li'l more original. Dat's too common," Goldie said. "Tonya, you got any suggestions?"

Tonya paused and thought hard for a second before she spoke. "Umm, how 'bout Tender? I like it 'cause it starts wit a T."

"Okay, sounds good ta me," Goldie said, seconding that nomination.

Kat added, "Yeah, dat's whut'z up! It kinda has a ring ta it."

It was a done deal. Now Tonya had an alias, her club name. Next, they put on some music and had Tonya—now Tender—do her thing. "Aiight. Let's see you move." Tender wasn't sure what they wanted. She did what she'd done for Todd, since he was the one that thought she had it going on. The young girl was really beautiful and could dance. Jackie's cousin had been right. Kat and Goldie looked at each other as they had the same thought. Tender had the goods to be the next hot flava at the clubs. ". . . Make eye contact." Goldie told her. "And always keep smilin'. No matter what bothers you or how scared you is . . ." Goldie and Kat were impressed. They spent the next few hours breaking down the language of the strip world and getting her ready for her debut.

TENDER WOULD RECEIVE her baptism by fire at Wild Things, a nightclub where anything goes: touching, fucking and sucking. No holds barred, if the price was right.

Goldie and Tender, chauffeured by Kat, pulled up in style in front of the club. They were late so they hurriedly grabbed their gear and processed into a jam-packed room thumping with the music of Biggie Smalls. There seemed to Tender to be as many dancers as there were customers. Making their way through the loud, smoke-filled hotspot was a task in itself. But they managed. They wouldn't have had to push through a crowd if Kat had been on time. Tender tried not to show it, but she was amazed at all the naked and half-naked dancers. It was all she could do to keep a straight face and not gawk.

Most of the girls were good-looking. A few were straight-up dogs, but had nice figures. A select few even had models' looks, with well-sculpted bodies, flat stomachs, nice breasts and nice fat asses. They were all shapes and sizes. There was someone for everyone here, no matter what their tastes were. Even an ugly female could make decent money if she had a personality to pull it off and was on top of her game as a dancer. But a dumb stripper would get played out every time.

They made their way to the dressing room, having pushed through a rowdy crowd of average hardworking Joes, hustlers, thugs and killers. The men were all shapes and sizes as well. More than a few of them noticed Tender and shouted out, "Shorty, hold up." Goldie held on to Tender's arm and told her to keep it moving. "No time for chitchat." The dressing room doors swung open and there in plain view were two bisexual strippers engaging in oral sex.

"Damn, Dynamite and Princess!" Goldie shouted. "Couldn't y'all wait till y'all got home? Y'all only live together." Tender's mouth fell open before she could catch herself. This open display of gayness struck Tender as strange. She knew there were girls like this in her school and on the street, but she'd never seen them getting down like this. It was not a pretty scene but it was one she had better get used to seeing. Seeing the sheer look of disgust on Tender's face, Goldie decided to pull her coat. "Get use to it! These bitches 'round here is off da chain. That ain't nuttin'. I seen a bitch stick a whole forty-ounce bottle of beer inside her pussy."

Kat laughed. "Yeah, da party just begun." In her new line of work, bisexuality was commonplace. Just being in the nude so much and around each other for days, weeks and months on end made some females curious, breaking down their defenses.

Kat didn't bat an eye. "Uh, huh. Get ya thing off, girl!" she coolly commented, "I know why two chicks could be gay? 'Cause pussy's so motherfuckin' good!"

Tender didn't know what to make of Kat's remark. Was she gay? Was she straight? Was she bisexual? Or was she curious? She made a mental note to keep a close eye on her.

With their privacy invaded, Dynamite and Princess stopped their own personal freak show for now. They'd finish up tonight, in the comfort of their apartment.

The girls quickly changed from their street clothes to their stripper outfits. Tender wore white hot pants with a matching see-through shirt and with white patent leather high-heel boots. Goldie and Kat both opted for g-strings with no tops. They left nothing to the imagination.

Kat reminded Tender again to smile, make eye contact. "Give them niggas lotsa conversation. Flirt wit 'em. Lie ta 'em. Lead 'em on. Make 'em think they da finest motherfucker in da club. Tell 'em anything ta get in their pockets. Then when da money run out, you roll out! Keep it movin', get dat paper . . . 'member, time iz money. So keep it movin'. You on da clock."

Tender received a crash course on driving men wild. This was just like cramming for a test, she thought. She had knots in her stomach and was unsure that she could retain all of their advice. The information seemed to be coming at her a mile a minute. She had to pick and choose what she could take in as well as what she could only think about later. Goldie noticed that she was nervous and distracted. She looked like a deer caught in the headlights of an oncoming car.

". . . Don't worry, Tender," Goldie reassured her, "one of us will always be by ya side. Holdin' you down, jus' in case . . ."

The butterflies flying in her stomach felt as if they were the size of bats. She worked to not let her feelings register in her facial expressions. Tonight was her coming-out party. And with a body like hers, she wouldn't go unnoticed.

Tender was like a breath of fresh air to the club, a delicacy in the meat market—or meat grinder—that was the strip club circuit. This was a machine that was always looking for youth to feed on the next new pretty face. The rule in this game was that as soon as a stripper's looks and body began to deteriorate, they were over. The machine chewed you up and spit you out. It was just a matter of time.

The women stepped out the dressing room and into the club. Though she wasn't alone, Tender felt like all eyes were on her. She felt a few hands sneaking free touches. She stepped straight to her business though, boldly asking a patron, "What's up, player? You tippin' or what?"

"Yeah," came the reply. He proceeded to feel all over her ass while he placed a dollar bill in the waistline of her hot pants.

"Wanna wall dance?" she inquired further.

He nodded his head.

This was her first customer. He handed over a twenty and backed up against the wall. Tender then turned around and pressed her ass up against his dick. She began throwing it on him, just as she did when she danced nasty at house parties. Like an octopus, he was all over her, his hands groping any part of her body that wasn't pressed up against him. As she picked up the speed, the more aroused he became, and he began stuffing bills everywhere. He was trying to hold back but he couldn't take it anymore; he let go of a nut. He felt like a sucker for coming in his pants but that's how hot Tender was.

Tender could feel the wetness even through his jeans. She realized she had overdone it. She was only supposed to take him to the brink, not have him actually climax. Your job was to leave men hanging, begging for more. She had failed at that.

She kept her eye on Goldie and Kat as much as she could from afar, mimicking everything they did. Goldie winked every so often, just to let her know she had her eye on her too. Tender thought to herself, Goldie is alright. There was something strange about the girl but she liked her. She seemed desperate for a friend. She also wore a small gold chain, with a crucifix attached, even while she danced. Tender considered this sort of sacrilegious, but she would mind her business and never offer a comment to Goldie.

The hours quickly passed. Soon it would be time for Tender's grand performance: her time up on stage, in the spotlight. Kat hadn't even told Tender. Each girl was able to do a solo performance. Tender had noticed that one by one the strippers appeared on the stage to do their thing for the room. She didn't think she would be doing the same.

Kat rushed to break the news to Tender. "You know it's almost ya turn to go up on stage?"

"What?" she responded. "I didn't know I had a turn."

"Yeah, we all do. I thought I told you that before," Kat said, knowing she was lying.

Goldie was nearby and hearing what Kat said, thought to herself, Here she goes with the bullshit again. Why can't she just be straight-up sometimes? She always gotta run game.

"Yo, I don't think I could do that," Tender said.

"Don't think like dat," Kat assured her. "You can do it. There ain't nuttin' to it. Besides ya regulars, dat's where most of ya dough comes from up in here."

Tender had watched all night while she worked as each girl did their thing. They shook their asses and even played with their pussies. Some freaked off, doing girl on girl numbers. They brought out the dog in every man in the house, as well as the dollars.

While Tender thought about it, Kat fumed. She took the girl's indecisiveness as an act of disobedience—something that she didn't tolerate in her clique. "Tender, you betta go out there and take them suckas' money," she said.

Goldie didn't have a problem with getting up on stage her first time around. She loved being the center of attention. All she had to do to get in the mood was to think about her father. This is what she did to get back at her father who abandoned her for his mistress and their son. When she danced, all she heard were compliments about her body, but all she saw was money, something that could take her farther than love, lust or revenge.

"Listen, Tender," Kat said, "If you don't get the fuck out there on dat stage, I don't know where your ass iz gonna stay tonight. But it won't be my house. Now you can either get up on dat stage or pack ya shit."

Goldie gave Kat a look that said, maybe she was going a bit too far. Goldie didn't like what she was saying, but she wouldn't challenge it.

Tender's heart sank. Wasn't Kat supposed to be cool peoples? Wasn't she suppose to be her homey? Then how could she issue an ultimatum like that?

"Aiight, I'll go."

Tender made her way to the stage. Just in time for the club's M.C. to announce her arrival.

"We got Tender comin' to da stage, to do her thing, wit her fine sexy self. Fellas, show some love. Come up off them dollars," he urged.

The DJ then put on one of the hottest songs out. It was one of those rump-shaker anthems. "Turn it around let me see something . . ." Mr. Cheeks rapped.

Tender smiled, but inside she felt thrown to the wolves without a weapon. She tried to keep her focus on the music and just dance. She looked randomly in the eyes of this, that and the other man standing in front of her. She was glad the DJ played a song she liked. She dipped and turned. She wound her hips. She panned the crowd with a pointed finger opening her arms like she was ready. By the lustful looks and the hooting and hollering, she must have been putting on a good show. She didn't give a fuck about these guys, they didn't know her struggle. They didn't count. She thought, I'm in this for the money. She imagined that she was alone in her room, dancing to the radio. The sex-starved crowd showered her with dollars and even bigger bills here and there. Goldie had to come on stage and help her gather up her loot.

Kat wore the smile of victory across her face, as she watched from the wings. She knew that Tender had it in her. All she had to do was push the right buttons. Desperation breeds a lot of things in the streets. When a person is fueled by it, there are no limits to how far one will go or what they will do.

After their set was over, Tender and Goldie gathered up all the scattered dollar bills that lay on the stage. They rushed back to the dressing room to refresh and regroup.

"Tender," Kat said as she entered the door beaming, "you wuz da bomb. Them niggas went crazy. They wuz sweatin' you hard as shit! . . ."

Tender smiled at her. But it was a front. She was not feeling Kat at all. Not after she flipped on her earlier. Kat was wrong.

Kat winked and hugged her, as if to say "I was joking earlier." Goldie was checking for Tender's reaction to Kat. Sensing some animosity in the air, Goldie said, "Yeah, Tender, you did do da damn thang! . . ."

TENDER WAS RELIEVED to finally be back at Kat's house. The night was long. Back home, while Kat was taking her shower, Tender and Goldie were free to kick it about everything that had happened.

"That was some real foul shit Kat said ta me," Tender said.

"She knows I'm in a jam. I'm pressed fa dough. My back iz against da wall."

". . . Yo, Tee, don't pay dat bitch no mind," Goldie said softly, referring to Kat. "She trip from time ta time. Just make ya loot and get da fuck away from her. *Run,* don't walk."

Tender was all ears now. What did Goldie mean by that? Aren't she and Kat supposed to be friends?

"What I'm telling you is between you and me. So keep dis on da down low," Goldie said. "You probably can't really understand what I'm sayin' or why I'm sayin' it. But if you stick around long enough, you'll see fa yaself."

In the distance they could hear the shower water cut off. They heard Kat heading in their direction. She was singing an old Mary J. Blige song aloud: "You remind of a love that I once knew . . ."

As they sat on her bed, Goldie reached out and squeezed Tender's hand. She began to talk loud as Kat came in earshot. ". . . Dat nigga wuz ugly, right?" They burst out laughing, trying to play it off.

"What y'all in here talking 'bout?" Kat asked, as she entered the bedroom.

"Aw, nuttin'," Goldie said. "Jus some lame-ass niggas who be tryin' ta cop a free feel."

"I be tellin' them broke-ass niggas all da time, hands off," Kat added. "Look fa free, touch for a small fee. You gotta put ya foot down wit these niggas, 'cause they got short arms and deep pockets. Let 'em touch you fa free if you want to and you'll be one broke bitch."

Goldie grinned at Kat, a big shit-eating smile, signaling her approval. In Kat's presence, Goldie said and did all the right things. To be around her was to be underneath her. Besides that, she always had to add her two cents to everything. Goldie was growing plain tired of all the extra stuff that Kat brought to the table.

". . . Dis one young nigga had been pressin' me fa some pussy fa da longest. I told 'em for two hundred dollars you can have all the pussy you want for a half hour . . . of course da nigga fronted afta I started talkin' 'bout paper. I said ta him you suppose to be ballin'? What, dat too rich fa ya blood? He looked at me like na. But at da same time he still tryin' ta jew me down. I'm like look nigga, treat yaself, don't beat yaself. My price iz what it iz! When you get a nickel over lunch money call me," Kat continued. ". . . I be doin' niggas dirty. Fuck 'em, they'd do it to me if I let 'em . . . I ain't lookin' fa love, I'm lookin' fa money. Hit me off! Na'mean?"

"You know, not every nigga in da club is foul," Goldie said. "Soma them are kinda nice. You just gotta weed 'em out. Fa real, fa real all I want is a nice lookin' dude wit a decent job and someone who will treat me right."

"Goldie, what you been smokin'?" Kat just shook her head. "I want soma dat. You must be crazy. I need more than what a nine to five nigga can provide fa me. Shit, I'll fuck around and blow his whole paycheck on teddies at Victoria's Secret. I needa nigga dat's gettin' serious cheddar. And I don't care how he gets it. Just break me off . . . But you don't think like me. Dat's why you'll neva get what I got. You on some ole Cinderella, happily ever after, fairy-tale bullshit . . ."

Money was Kat's man. That's what she wanted to maintain at all costs, even if that meant burning bridges or sabotaging her friendships.

So many dudes told her how good her pussy was. She thought it was lined with platinum.

Goldie wanted Tender to see how Kat really got down. "Damn, money ain't everything. I mean, what about romance? Commitment? A soul mate? True love? Huh? . . . I don't know about you but one day I'ma settle down and get married. And then have some kids."

"Me and a broke-ass nigga ain't gonna work," Kat insisted.

"What can he do fa me except bring me down. You say money ain't everything, ta me it's da only thing. Money makes da world go 'round. But besides dat, you ain't gonna find no Prince Charming or Mr. Right in no strip club! It ain't gonna happen. These ain't da type of niggas dat go to church on Sunday. These niggas come ta da club wit one thing on their mind, *pussy!* At da end of da night, dem niggas iz lined up, waitin' ta see who they can slide off wit."

"All dat's fine and dandy, but I'm not gonna be a stripper too long. Dis shit is takin' it's toll on me already," Goldie shot back.

"Yeah, yeah!" Kat said sarcastically. "I've heard dat before. But you still strippin', ain't you? You ain't goin' nowhere."

"Says who?" Goldie said. "Says me!" Kat replied. Then shot her an evil eye, to let her know she meant business and not to push her luck.

Goldie was in serious violation of Kat's rules. She knew better than to be running off at the mouth, Kat thought. Didn't Goldie know? Or did she forget that things had to be her way or you hit the highway?

A voice inside Goldie was saying, "Hold up. Let it ride. Don't spoil things for Tender." Plus she already proved the point she was trying to make to the young girl.

"Anyway," Goldie said, shrugging it off. "You right. I am all talk and no action . . . But yo, did you see how dat broad Precious was following you 'round da club?"

Goldie let Kat think she won. That she had killed her dream. Sooner or later, Goldie promised herself she was getting out the game, one way or another. Kat could say or think whatever she wanted to.

"Yeah, I peeped dat stink ho!" Kat acknowledged her. "She wanna be me so bad it's ridiculous. I think I'ma start callin' her Mini-Me . . . Dat raggedy pussy bitch be tryin ta cock-block too. She hate ta see me get money. She fuckin' behind me. Anybody I fucked, she try and fuck. If I was a nigga, I wouldn't give da ho a dime, let alone a dollar . . . She must give bomb head, 'cause her pussy is tore up from da floor up. You see how big and nasty lookin' her shit is. Yuck! . . ."

". . . Somebody needs ta tell her she ain't built like dat fa dis shit. She's a hamburger away from da fat farm," Kat said, hating. "Low budget ho! Dat bitch'll fuck for a buck. And do somethin' strange for some change."

Cutting her off, Goldie asked, "You see them fake-ass pimps in da club tanite?"

"Yeah," Kat replied. "I peeped them." Turning to Tender she said, "Don't give them niggas no rap either. Tender, I'm tellin' you, on everything I love, they gonna try you. They'll come at you wit promises, talkin' 'bout they can do dis and dat fa you. How they'll make you their bottom bitch and you'll have dis, dat and a third."

Tender asked a question. "What's a bottom bitch?" she innocently inquired.

Goldie interjected, "Jus' another word fa a pimp's main ho. See, da pimp gets rich, while all you get is da dick. Lots of it."

"We don't have pimps up in here. . . . They call us renegades," Kat announced proudly. "'Cause we don't get down wit they program. 'Cause we won't be a part of nobody's stable . . . Shit, I know how ta pimp myself, I don't need no middle man pimpin' me. Dat's fa them weak bitches who need to feel wanted or a part of somethin'. Fuck dat, 'cause when my pussy gets sore from fuckin', I'ma give it a break. And ain't no nigga gonna beat me or press me ta fuck when I don't feel like it!"

Goldie yawned and stretched. "I'm tired!" she mumbled.

"Me, too!" Kat agreed, as she got up and proceeded to her room. "I'll see y'all when I wake up, if I wake up."

"Later," Tender managed to say.

"Nite! Nite!" Goldie cracked. She turned to Tender. "See, I

told you she got some shit wit her. And it ain't all good." She paused. "Dat's enuff excitement fa da day. I'm goin' ta bed."

"Good night, Goldie," Tender said. "Good lookin' out! Thanks fa everything."

Tender tucked herself into the bed. In her corner of the room, Goldie got on her knees. She touched the crucifix that she was wearing around her neck, and silently said a long prayer, like she did every night. She paused in front of a picture of her mother on her night table. She made the sign of the cross. Then she went into a drawer and pulled out a navy blue diary. She opened its lock and made quick notes in it. She wrote her confessions. She hoped this would cleanse her of her sins.

# 3

GLORIA, VENA QUI! (Gloria, c'mere)" Ms. Cruz called out to her daughter, as she entered the apartment, returning home from school. Though Ms. Cruz spoke fluent English, she preferred to speak in her native tongue whenever possible.

Gloria detected a sense of urgency in her mother's voice. She yelled back, "Comin', Ma." And she wondered what was wrong. Before making her way back to her mother's room, she stopped and put some leftovers from last night's dinner in the oven. She was starving.

Gloria walked past the living room, as she glanced in at her mother's shrine to the Virgin mother Mary and Jesus Christ. The off-white living room walls were bare except for a huge, beautifully painted picture of a Caucasian, blue-eyed Jesus, with sunrays from the heavens descending brightly upon him. Next to that was an equally beautiful picture of the Virgin Mary. She was Ms. Cruz's shinning example of purity. This was all that a woman should strive for. Accompanying the two portraits were numerous burning candles, holy water and blessed beads.

Ms. Cruz was a devout Roman Catholic. She lived her life as if the world were coming to an end today. When the saints came marching in, she wanted to be among the chosen few that made it into those pearly gates of heaven. She wanted the same for her only child.

Gloria went to her room and saw that her mother was sitting on the edge of the bed, watching her daily dose of soap operas and chain-smoking Newport cigarettes. She loved cigarettes and soap operas to death. Her day just wouldn't go right without one of the two. While smoking relaxed her, soap operas allowed her entrance into a glamorous, sometimes scandalous lifestyle that she could only imagine.

Ms. Cruz was pregnant with Gloria when she came to the United States from Puerto Rico. She was a young woman who had shamed her family by running off with an older lover, Felipe. It was he who brought her to the United States and to Philadelphia. North Philly became Cruz's home away from home and it was here that she raised her only child. She was now laid off from her factory job and frustrated with collecting unemployment checks.

"¿*Que es esto?* (What's this?)" Ms. Cruz asked, as she thrust a stack of envelopes toward her. Her mother had found the love letters that her boyfriend, Angel "Green Eyes" Lopez, had written to her while he was in jail.

Ms. Cruz had forbidden her daughter from seeing Lopez, or any other boy, after catching them walking home from school together. He was a handsome young man. She knew from the moment she laid eyes on "Green Eyes" that he was nothing but trouble for her daughter. She felt it in her gut, and she was right. He was a ladies' man. He was average height, a solid muscular build, dark curly hair, with a sandy brown complexion. His pearly white teeth and emerald green eyes made him stand out. He was a drug dealer, and a baby maker. He fathered a half a dozen children by as many women by the ripe old age of nineteen.

All the neighborhood girls were well aware of his hit-and-run style, everyone except for Gloria. Her mother had sheltered her from the streets and literally, at times, locked her inside the house. She prayed profusely over her. She did all this yet failed to teach her daughter about the facts of life.

So Gloria was easy pickings for "Green Eyes." He charmed her, she fell in love and was blinded by her feelings. She was willing to defy anyone and anything to be with him, including her mother and her covenant with God.

"*¿No te dije que dejaras a ese muchacho?* (Didn't I tell you to leave that boy alone?)" Ms. Cruz yelled. Her voice rose and her face turned red. "*¡El no es bueno para ti! ¡El es el Diablo! ¿Intiendes? El no es nada mas que un pajaro cárcel.* (He's no good for you! He's the devil! Understand? He's nothing but a jailbird.)"

Salty tears began to flow down Gloria's cheeks and into the corners of her mouth.

"But Mommy, that's not true!" Gloria explained. "You don't know him like I know him. He's a good person."

Ms. Cruz shook her head in disbelief. She never thought she'd live to see the day when her daughter would openly defy her. Ms. Cruz took another long drag on her cigarette and then aimed it at her daughter. The glowing tip of the cigarette touched the girl's skin.

Gloria was in shock. Her mother continued jabbing at her with the cigarette, backing the girl into a corner. It took a moment for her to grasp what was happening and protect herself. This was her mother.

"Mama. Don't."

"*¿Con quien tu te Crees que estas hablando?* (Who do you think you are talking to?)" Ms. Cruz exploded. "*¿Estas loca? ¡Yo,* *soy tu madre! Yo a tite di a luz.* ¡*Y Antes que te Veo runiar tu vida,* *primero yo te mato! Ese muchacho no es bueno.* (You crazy? I am your mother! I gave birth to you. And before I see you ruin your life, I'll kill you first! That boy is no good.)"

"But Mommy, I love him!"

"¡*Tu no sabes nada del amor!* ¡*Tu eres un bebe!* (You know nothing about love! You are a baby! What do you know about love? Huh?)"

They stood a few feet apart, like two gunslingers at high noon. Ms. Cruz was breathing heavily, while Gloria wrapped her arms around herself and rocked back and forth in a vain effort to shake off the pain she was feeling from the burns.

"Look at what you've done to me, Mommy; because some-body—he loves me too." She announced, "We're gonna be married, Mommy." All this and her mother didn't even know that she was pregnant.

"¡*Tu eres una malagradecia Puta!* (You ungrateful bitch!)" She cursed. "¡*Yo te voy a matar! Sobre mi cardave, te dejo casarte con ese muchacho.* (I'm gonna kill you! Over my dead body will you marry that boy.)"

"Then you're going to kill me and your unborn grandchild," Gloria blurted out. Ms. Cruz had a wild look in her eyes. She was frozen for a moment. But then she picked up a lamp that rested on her night table and hurled it at her daughter. Gloria ducked. A split second after, the lamp hit the wall and shattered. It landed inches away from where Gloria's head had been.

Gloria moved with quickness, now really fearing for her life. She scrambled to her feet and bolted out the room. She stumbled through the apartment, bumping into everything in her path.

"¡*Gloria, ven par tras!* (Gloria, come back here!)" her mother cried. The girl could not hear her now.

• • •

GLORIA RAN STRAIGHT to Green Eyes's room. "I can't believe ya own mother did this to you!" He cleaned up her wounds. "She loco fa real! Man, I wish I wuz there. I woulda . . . Dat ain't ya fuckin' mother if she did you like that. Dat's a fuckin' monster."

"Green Eyes, don't say those things," she begged. "She didn't mean to do it. I know she didn't. She snapped. She's still my mother," Gloria cried.

Green Eyes's blood was boiling. From the moment Gloria walked in the door and collapsed in his arms, he wanted to punish whoever did this to his girl. This situation called for revenge.

"Nah, Gloria," he insisted. "I don't care what you say, dat bitch ain't ya mother. Not doin' shit like dat. Fa Christ sake, ya her only child and she do you like that? Hell fuckin' no! . . ."

Green Eyes jumped off the bed and stormed to his closet. Then he began to frantically search for something. Going through old sneaker boxes, he discarded each one till he finally found what he was looking for. He pulled out a black .380 semi-automatic handgun. He gripped the weapon and turned around, walking back toward his girlfriend.

"Here!" he said, as he extended the gun toward her.

Gloria froze up, as if she were hypnotized by the gun. She stared blankly at it for what seemed to be an eternity, unsure of what to say or do.

"Wha, what's dat for?" she stuttered.

"Here!" he repeated angrily, as he stared evilly at her. "Dis for you. Go straighten out ya mother."

"What?" Gloria asked unbelievably. "I can't . . ."

Green Eyes wasn't gonna take no for an answer. He wanted her out of his way, for once and for all. "Either you do it or I'll do it," he told her. "If I do it, I'ma use a knife. I'ma poke so many holes in her, she's gonna look like Swiss cheese. I'm gonna make her suffer for all the bad things she ever had to say about me. . . ."

Numb, out of her mind, Gloria took the gun and marched out the door. She rather than Green Eyes. He was as crazy as her mom.

MS. CRUZ WAS SCOURING the room for another cigarette. Finding them among debris on the floor, she began to pat herself down, looking for her lighter. She found it and placed a cigarette in her mouth. She hadn't noticed the smell of gas vapors from the kitchen stove that filtered the air. She was too drunk with anger at her daughter and herself. She flicked the lighter and its flame became a fireball.

GLORIA WALKED IN A DAZE, unaware of anyone or anything on the mean streets of North Philly. The people and places she passed on the way home were a blur to her. She looked at nothing and no one. She tried to visualize aiming a gun at her mother but couldn't. She didn't know what she was going to do next. She just knew she had to keep Green Eyes and her mother apart.

People in the neighborhood thought that another bombing incident had occurred. The sight of fire and smoke took them back to the time when the Philadelphia city government bombed the headquarters of MOVE, an African-American organization of militants. The explosion and the fire it caused wiped out an entire city block, causing loss of life and property damage in the millions.

GREEN EYES WAS NOW all Gloria had left and life with him became a living hell. Now he beat on her. It didn't matter to him that she was pregnant. He forgot that he was ready to kill Gloria's mother because she had beaten the girl.

She told herself that this was God's punishment of her. She

didn't have other friends or family to turn to. She tried to accept her fate. Green Eyes came in one day, mad because of a hustle and stomped on her stomach. She ended up in the hospital. The kick triggered her to hemorrhage. She lost the baby that day. Green Eyes picked her up from the hospital with plenty of "I'm sorry" on his tongue. He tried to hug up on her and said everything's going to be alright. But she knew that nothing about the situation was nice. She couldn't take the sight of him anymore. Like a thief in the night, she snuck out the house and vanished into the night . . . She took with her only the clothes on her back.

Life on the street was rough, but it was better than living with him. She slept on the steps of a church for a few nights until the police took notice. She had to sleep with one eye open and one eye closed. But that was better than being a human punching bag. As fate would have it, one night while roaming the Greyhound bus station in Center City, Gloria would meet someone who would change her life forever.

"Excuse me, mister," she began. "I'm homeless and hungry. If you would be so kind and spare some change it would be greatly appreciated. . . ."

The old white man just ignored her and kept walking. He was very wary to whom he gave his hard-earned money. One never could tell who was on drugs these days. He left her standing there looking stupid. At the same time, another stranger overheard the conversation and came to her aid.

"Here you go," she said, placing a twenty-dollar bill in her hand.

"God bless you," Gloria replied. "Thank you, miss."

"Is it true? What you told dat man 'bout you bein' homeless?" Kat inquired. Kat had noticed Gloria, thinking that even though she was dressed like a bum, she was beautiful. She was pretty enough to be any man's wife. And yet she was living like this.

Gloria was reluctant to talk to her. She answered with a look.

"Come on, I'll buy you a soda." Gloria nodded and followed Kat. "Where you from?" Kat asked, stepping up to a self-serve soda fountain. "Let's sit down." Kat motioned to a bench.

"Why you being nice to me?"

"Well," Kat said, "you look like you've had a hard time and don't deserve it. You out here, but you look too good for me to think you been out here long. I might be able to help you."

"Help me?" Gloria looked doubtful.

"What's your story?" Kat asked.

Kat was in the station because she had worked a private party in New York. When she saw Gloria it occurred to her that she could find girls to work the parties with her. What better women than those who needed somebody to have their back. Fuck a pimp getting a piece of the piece a woman sells. She wanted an alliance of women like herself who needed to hustle but didn't want to be under any man's rule.

In Gloria, Kat saw someone so down in the dumps that she could mold and control her.

"If you want to, you can come stay wit me, at my crib. I gotta extra room," Kat offered. Gloria hesitated but Kat could see the joy already registering all across Gloria's face.

"Fa real?"

"Fa real!" Kat replied. "You too pretty to be livin' like dis. There's all types of shit you could be doin' ta get paid. I'ma show you how ta make some 'real' money."

Gloria wanted to ask what she meant by that but she didn't say anything. No matter what Kat was offering it was more than she had at the moment. Together they hopped in a cab and headed straight to Kat's house. Kat had a gut feeling that this was the best twenty dollars she ever invested.

# 4

A GROUP OF YOUNG KIDS sat on an abandoned row house stoop on 45th Street and Aspen Avenue, exhausted after playing a game of tag. As they chilled, they began to crack jokes on each other. They quickly went from jokes about each other to mother insults.

". . . Ya mother loved Skippy peanut butter so much she skipped school," one boy cracked.

"Ya mother's so nasty," another commented, "she puts ice in her draws to keep da crabs fresh."

Back and forth they went exchanging insult for insult, much to the delight of the onlookers. They laughed up a storm at these vulgar jokes. But one boy in particular, Kat's son, Eric, laughed a little too hard and a little too long, for one kid's liking.

"What you laughin' at, Eric?" the kid asked, taking offense. "It wasn't dat motherfuckin' funny, nigga!"

Doubled over in laughter, Eric tried to ignore him but the kid put a strong enough emphasis on his statement that it was like he was calling him out.

"Nigga, what da fuck iz so funny?" he asked again. "I know you ain't laughin'? At least my mother ain't no fuckin' stripper! Dat's how she got dat fat-ass truck. And how you get ya gear. Ya mother shows her ass, all fuckin' night. Now, nigga, how ya like dat? Let's see if you find dat so funny."

"Shut da fuck up, nigga!" Eric demanded. "You don't know what da fuck you talkin' 'bout. My mother ain't no stripper. You betta take dat back."

The boy laughed. "Yeah, right! Sure she ain't . . . I ain't takin' nuttin' back! It's true, whether you know it or not. Nigga, da joke's on you . . ."

"Take dat back!" Eric insisted again. "Stop lyin' on my mother."

The boy continued, "Why you don't live wit ya mother? Huh? How come she only comes ta visit but never stays over? . . . Cause she can't! She works in da strip club at night. E'rybody knows too, my big brother told me . . ."

Eric's eyes were watering as his temper was rising. He spoke with his fists. He pummeled the boy to the ground.

"Don't talk about my mother like dat! Take it back! Nigga! Take it back! . . ." Eric ordered him, as he connected with punch after punch. It happened so fast the other kids barely had time to react. Seeing that the fight was one-sided they quickly broke it up, not wanting to see a fight among friends.

NICOLE CARTER, affectionately known as Ms. Nicky, was presiding over one of her weekend marathon card games. All night long, she and her girlfriends drank hard liquor, chain-smoked cigarettes, traded insults and stayed at each other's throats over small amounts of money wagered. It was as much of a social event as it was a card game.

". . . You know who had the nerve to bring they ass 'round

here?" Ms. Nicky stated to nobody in particular as she held her cards close to her chest. "That no-good nigga, Reds."

"What that nigga want?" someone asked, further fueling the conversation. Another lady replied, "What they all want?"

"Pussy!" they all seemed to say in unison.

"That fool gotta one-track mind," Ms. Nicky said. "Jus' lika young boy. But I shut 'em down. Ain't nuttin' happenin', I told 'em. Like that old song says, ain't no romance witout finance. You gotta have a J-O-B, if you wanna be wit me . . . I can do bad by myself. I don't need no lazy, grown-ass man, layin' up in my bed and not contributin' to my household . . . Shit, that nigga must be on that shit if he think he comin' up in here wit that non-sense. . . ."

Ms. Nicky and her daughter, Katrina, were just alike in more ways than one. You could see, by the short and tight outfits she wore, she desperately wanted to hold on to her youth. Aside from physically looking alike, they shared the same ideology and mentality. She schooled Kat that it was better to be the user than to be used. She wanted Kat to do as she said, not as she had done.

Eric came running through the kitchen like a train. He knew better than to do that in his grandmother's house.

"Hey! Hey!" she called out to the blur that just passed her. "Eric! You musta lost ya God damn mind, runnin' through my house like that! . . . Bring ya li'l ass back here and walk like you got some sense."

Ignoring his grandmother, Eric continued to hightail it through the house and up the steps to his room. He slammed his door shut and threw himself on the bed and cried his eyes out.

Ms. Nicky knew that something must be wrong. "I'll be right back!" she said as she got up and left the card table. She was going to give her grandson a beating for disrespecting her in front of her company. This really wasn't like him, though. He actually had more respect or fear for her than he did his own mother. It was she who raised him, who disciplined him.

". . . Can we at least finish this hand?" someone asked. The request fell on deaf ears. Ms. Nicky kept right on going.

Marching upstairs to his room, Ms. Nicky flung his door open. "What the hell is wrong with you, boy?" she demanded to know. "It betta be good too! 'Cause I should beat the black off ya ass for showin' off."

Still sobbing, Eric rolled over on his back. His grandmother could see the hurt and pain in his face. "Nana . . ." He began to babble. He said somethin' bad 'bout my momma." "I was fightin' him . . . I wanted ta kill 'im! . . ."

She sat down on the bed. Kids could be mean, she thought, and it was no secret what Kat did for a living. "You mean ta tell me you came runnin' through my house like a madman, trackin' up my fuckin' kitchen floor, cause some li'l no good, black bastard said somethin' 'bout ya damn mother?" she asked. "I'ma whip ya motherfuckin' ass! . . ."

"But Nana, he said my mother's a stripper! And that's how she can afford to buy me nice stuff—"

"So da fuck what!" she exploded. "I wouldn't give a damn what that li'l son of a bitch said. I don't care if he said ya mother was Santa Claus. You shoulda told the cocksucker to mind his own business. And worry 'bout how his momma get his shit. He don't know what his momma gotta do to put food in his mouth and clothes on his back . . . That's why black-on-black crime so high now, 'cause niggas don't mind they business. I swear! . . ."

As his grandmother ranted and raved, he noticed that she never once denied that his mother was a stripper. His heart hurt with shame.

"Stay right here, boy! Don't move. I'm callin' ya mother over here right now, to talk to you." The woman knew her daughter well and knew that Kat felt she didn't owe anybody an explana-

tion for her actions. But as far as Ms. Nicky was concerned, she
had to answer to her son.

MS. NICKY CALLED KAT, telling her she needed to come
now and deal with her child. Kat arrived an hour later. She
turned over in her mind the entire drive over just what she would
say to him. Where would she begin?

"Mom." Eric smiled as his mother walked into his room. Just
the sight of her lifted his spirits.

"Hey, li'l man," she greeted him. "What's dis I hear 'bout you
fightin' and carryin' on 'round here? And what did I tell you 'bout
dat cryin' mess? Huh? . . ." His eyes were still red and the traces
of tears were on his face.

". . . Cryin' fa girls!" he said, echoing his mother's sentiments.
If she wanted a weak son, she would have had a daughter, she always said. She knew growing up in Philly—the hood—where
only the strong survived.

"That's right!" she agreed. "Be strong. Don't cry . . . You hear
me? . . . Well, did you win da fight?"

"Yeah, Ma, I won! I hit 'im like dis," he stated confidently,
while showing off the boxing combinations his mother had
taught him.

"Good, because if you didn't, I'm takin' you right back out
there ta fight 'im again."

She was trying to be tough on him yet at the same time gentle.
She walked a fine line. Such was the life of a single mom in the
hood trying to raise a strong black man.

"But Ma," Eric explained. "I got so mad . . . afta he said you
was a stripper. I just 'membered hearin' bad things 'bout them
. . . And I know you not bad . . . So when he said that . . ."

"Listen, Eric," Kat said gently, as she looked deeply into her
son's innocent eyes, "I'm not a stripper. . . ." Kat lied, in an effort
to soften the blow. "I'ma exotic dancer. . . ."

Shifting gears, she said, "Eric, lemme ask you somethin'. If I wuz a bum in da street, would you love me any less?"

"No," he quickly replied.

"If I was a WNBA basketball player, would you love me any more?" she questioned.

"No," came the answer again. "I'll love 'cause . . . 'cause you my mommy."

"Good!" She smiled. "'Cause Mommy gotta do what she gotta do, to take good care of you. I'll do *anything* and *everything* to make sure my baby has . . . Don't you like da nice things Mommy buys you?"

"Yeah," Eric, answered. "You always get 'em fa me first. Before any of my friends have 'em."

"Well, Eric, those things are expensive," she insisted. "They cost money. And Mommy makes her money dancing. It's my job. Just like any other parent has a job . . ." She went on convincing her son of the legitimacy of her line of work. ". . . My job is no different from anybody else's. My money spends just like theirs."

"I know strippers take off all they clothes. Do exotic dancers do dat? . . ." he asked. "Can't you get another job? Where you could work in da morning and come home in da aftanoon? Dat way I could see you more . . ."

"Eric, all I do is dance on stage with my bathing suit on. I don't take off my clothes. And yes, I could get another job. But this pays a lot more. So for da time bein', we, me and you have to sacrifice. Sacrifice not seein' each other so much now, so dat Mommy can make more money and we can live better, and together, later . . . Wouldn't you like dat?"

"Yeah," he said excitedly, smiling. Just the thought of finally living with his mother brought a smile to his face. He threw his arms around her neck, hugging and kissing her. She held him close for a moment. He was proud to have her for his mommy. No matter what anybody said.

"I love you, Ma," Eric whispered. "You da best mommy in da whole entire world."

Kat fought back a tear. She flashed back to a memory of her own childhood, and all the love she never received.

KATRINA CARTER grew up in a single parent household in the hood. And like so many other young children there, she was exposed to the street life at an early age. Her mother was a barfly, a party animal. Oftentimes, Nicky left Kat and her older sister Jackie home alone while she went out. Her children came to her more like a big sister than a mother. They basically grew up at their grandmother's house anyway. A female might have birthed Kat, but it was clear the streets raised her. Her mother spent too much time in after-hour spots, speakeasies, clubs and hustlers' beds, to rightfully tend to them. And when that played out, she began to strip.

"The world ain't no place fa an old ho!" Nicky often said. "So if you gonna be a ho, be a good one. Make ya money while ya still young. Get paid! And hopefully if ya lucky, you'll marry a nigga wit some damn money. Don't marry no broke nigga, then come back 'round here lookin' fa a handout. 'Cause I ain't got nuttin' fa ya. Ya hear me . . . I'm serious! Once y'all get eighteen, y'all on ya own. So ya betta marry fa money. You can always learn ta love 'em later . . . If ya gonna fuck, don't fuck fa free . . . These men will use you, till they can't use you no more. Talk about you, then throw you away like yesterday's newspaper . . ."

"I dare you ta break dat window," Kat's friend Tom urged. He was eleven years old, just like her.

"You dare me?" Kat repeated.

"I double-dare you," Toni said, raising the stakes.

Feeding into her friend's suggestion, Kat picked up a brick and hurled it into a neighbor's living room window. She was identified and caught minutes later.

". . . Why da hell did you break that old lady's window?" her mother demanded to know. "She ain't neva done nuttin' ta you. So what made you do dat?"

"Umm, Toni told me ta do it," she said.

"Toni told you ta do it, huh? Well you can thank Toni fa dis ass whuppin' you 'bout ta get. Afta I'm finished tearin' ya ass up, you'll neva listen to her or anybody else again! Now, hurry up and take off those clothes. I'ma cut dat ass . . ."

With that, Ms. Carter proceeded to make good on her promise. She beat the living daylights out of her daughter. When she did stop, it was because she had somewhere to go. From that day on, Kat knew to lead, not follow. Over and over again Nicky Carter told her, "If ya gonna be an Indian, be a chief!"

# 5

F RIDAY NIGHTS WERE JUMPING at the Bottoms Up club. Any stripper in her right mind would be there on the week-end. This was when the "real" money was made, when the play-ers came out to play.

Tender, Goldie and Kat, inside the dressing room, began their transformation from regular women to sexy strippers. More and more Tender sought to distinguish herself from the rest by wear-ing something different. She had learned to play a role when she performed. She got into rocking a short nurse's uniform, a con-struction worker's outfit, complete with lunch box, hard hat and orange fluorescent safety vest, and other fantasy dress. By going the extra mile, she drew a lot of attention to herself.

She got a lot of play, even without the costumes. The atmo-sphere among the dancers in strip clubs is competition in that there are those who try to be "that Bitch," the star. There were strippers who stood out, turned heads for various reasons. Their facial beauty, body or charm got some notice. Then there were those who just sparkled like a diamond for no particular reason. Tender was among those who naturally shined.

Haters began to spring up left and right from close and far away. Kat seemed to think that all the money Tender spent on outfits was a waste. And she told her so. But Tender didn't feel that way. She kept right on doing it, spending her money on what she liked. The other strippers in the club hated on Tender, mostly because of the company she was keeping. Kat was known for having a big mouth, sharp tongue and arrogance. Kat's clique tolerated her because they owed her.

"Whatcha wearin' tanite?" Kat asked Tender. She was slipping into a skimpy red, white and blue outfit that almost made her resemble Wonder Woman.

"You'll see," Tender replied, as she pulled up her black fishnet stocking.

Goldie interjected, "Tender, I don't give a fuck whatcha wearin'! Ta each his own."

Goldie didn't particularly care to get all dressed up in an outfit only to have to take it all off anyway. She opted to wear a black thong with matching stilettos. Tender and Kat continued to dress, ignoring Goldie's remark. More and more, whenever Goldie was involved in a conversation that had anything to do with stripping, she automatically turned negative. It was like she was letting everyone around her with a pair of ears know she could care less about being here. She didn't belong here. She was unhappy.

"I'm gone," Kat announced, grabbing her clutch purse. "It's money out there. And I know them niggas iz horny and drunk and feelin' real generous."

Before she could leave the dressing room, in walks another stripper named Cookie with the exact same outfit on. Kat was instantly pissed. She began to talk loudly.

"Bitches, ain't gotta original bone in their body." She spat, pretending to be talking to her clique. "I hate a copycat, na'mean? Bitches too busy trying to be me. Insteada doin' them."

Cookie shot her an icy stare, but said nothing. She realized she was outnumbered right now. All her home girls were in the club working. Now was not the time to be brave.

It was no secret that Kat hated Cookie with a passion. They had had numerous run-ins with each other over the years, over everything from stolen items to mutual customers and matching outfits. What Kat really couldn't stand about her was the fact that people kept telling her how much they looked alike. She thought they only said this because they both were light-skinned with light eyes. To her, that's where the similarities began and ended. Kat thought she looked better than her, straight up and down.

Somehow they always seemed to bump heads. Kat felt like she was trying to steal her style. She was stepping on her toes purposely. Imitation may have been the sincerest form of flattery but not in Kat's book. Several times she stepped to Cookie about it. They ended up damn near fighting—but nothing changed. If anything, the situation escalated. Kat was a hothead. It didn't take much to light her fuse. Cookie wasn't really a threat to her. Kat knew she could mop the floor with her. The biggest threat to Kat would come from within her own clique.

Yet another reason why Kat disliked Cookie was because she was a prostitute. When she first got into the game of stripping, it was Cookie who tried to pull her into her pimp's stable. Kat saw through their shenanigans. She didn't need nobody to pimp her because she wanted all the profits for herself. Why work like a dog all year round in all kinds of weather, only to hand over your hard-earned money to somebody who didn't help her make it. To her, all the pimps and streetwalkers who had infiltrated the club scene were messing up the game—her hustle. As a result of her rejecting their offer, Kat and any other girl who didn't fall under a pimp's umbrella were labeled renegades. A title she wore proudly. Tender was puzzled by the whole situation. She didn't know the details of Kat and Cookie's history, so she just stayed quiet, playing it by ear.

"Let da track hos stay on da track. And da clubs hos stay in da club! You bitches iz in da way," Kat barked, directing that insult at Cookie. "You can hate me now but I won't stop now . . ." She chanted the hit record by rapper Nas as she sashayed out of the locker room.

The girls watched as Cookie slammed her locker shut. She was visibly upset. Goldie then turned and whispered to Tender, "Girl, be on point tanite. You see dat look on her face? She's tight! She gotta li'l gully-ass mob up in here too. So somethin' might jump off . . . I don't know why dat bitch Kat sounded her like dat. But she always set shit off witout thinkin' 'bout da repercussions . . . Anyway, like I said, keep ya eyes open and watch ya back . . ."

LOOKING LIKE A WOMAN of ill repute from the prohibition era, Tender took to the stage in a red micro-mini skirt with matching long black satin gloves and a feather in her hair.

On cue, Tender began to dance to one of her favorite rap songs, "What Y'all Niggas Want," by Philadelphia rap star Eve. She had to hit the DJ off with a little something extra to make sure the songs she liked to dance to got played while she was on stage. She had become a professional crowd pleaser.

All around Tender were at least half a dozen other dancers doing their thing. But all eyes were focused on her. She had star quality. In a few short months she had mastered the art of strip-tease.

The gymnastic training she got in school now came in handy. She could work the pole. She could climb it, then extend her legs into a split. She could interlock her legs around the pole, bending backward, and slide down the pole into a handstand. She left the other strippers in awe. Out the corner of their eyes, they watched to see what she would do next.

After reaching the ground and getting back on her feet, slowly, Tender unfastened her outfit and seductively dropped it to the floor. Now, she was nude, except for her thigh-high fishnet stockings, stilettos, and gloves. Having completely captivated her audience, she bent over using the pole for support. Individually, she began to make her ass cheeks bounce. She then elegantly dropped to the floor spreading her legs wide, giving every man a full view of her neatly shaved vagina. Playfully, she touched it, fueling their frenzy. She flip-flopped into various poses. She crawled on all fours. She even jumped on the bar and gave some lucky guy an up close and personal peep show. He got his jollies off by feeling her up every time he placed a bill in her stocking.

At this point the DJ hollered into the mic, "Dis ain't a free show! Tip da lady!"

The customers willingly obliged, lavishly tossing money at her.

As Tender wrapped up her show and gathered up her money, she glanced around the club for Goldie and Kat. She spotted Goldie in the corner giving some dude a lap dance. But Kat wasn't anywhere in sight. Maybe she's using the bathroom or VIPing with a customer, she mused.

Tender heard loud voices as she rushed back to the dressing room to freshen up before she came out to work the crowd.

"Bitch, you had a lot mouth earlier. Where's all dat slick shit you wuz sayin' now? Huh? Can't front witout ya friends?" Tender paused to see who was talking. It was Cookie.

"Ho, you heard what the fuck I said!" Kat spat. "I ain't gonna bite my tongue. You's a fake-ass, low-budget, wannabe me. Did you hear dat?"

Kat was surrounded by the enemy—four rough ghetto girls. But she wasn't about to give them the satisfaction of chumping her. As soon as the words left her mouth, she hauled off and punched Cookie, the closest to her.

Cookie's head whipped back violently from the blow. She was caught off guard. Instantly, her friends pounced on Kat.

Tender turned on her heels to find Goldie, who was giving a lap dance to a guy. Tender snatched her off the customer's lap and pulled her toward the dressing room.

"Hey, hey!" The guy jumped up.

"What's wrong?" Goldie asked, not missing a beat, following Tender wherever she was taking her.

"Kat's getting jumped!" After she said that, Tender noticed a subtle resistance from Goldie. She made a mental note of Goldie's hesitation but continued on. Before reaching the dressing room, Tender grabbed a half empty bottle of Heineken that stood abandoned on one of the tables.

Kat was tussling with Cookie when they stepped in. The other three girls took turns sucker punching her. Tender sprung into action like a bat out of hell and joined the melee, trying to break the Heineken bottle on somebody's head.

Goldie, in the meantime, was issuing love taps. She was only trying to do enough to say she helped and not much more.

"Get off her!" Goldie shouted. The woman had begun to get back anyway. Tender was in shape, strong and fast. Kat didn't have enough though. It wasn't over till she got all the licks she wanted in. She initiated round two, taking wild swings at her opponents. She was mad enough to seriously hurt somebody. In a blink of an eye, chairs went flying and there were bites, scratches and screams. Hair extensions, tracks and blood lay on the floor.

All the commotion in the locker room drew the attention of the club's bouncers, who came in and separated the two parties as the women continued to toss threats back and forth between them.

Kat was pleasantly surprised to know that Tender had that

much fight in her. She wondered if she could beat Tender in a fair one.

THE GIRLS SAT AROUND a bedroom at home that night reliving the fight and nursing their wounds. "How dare they move on me like that? Them bum-ass bitches couldn't even jump me right," Kat bragged. "They wuz hittin' each other more than they did me . . . I swear da next time I see dat fuckin' slut Cookie, it's on and poppin'! . . . She could be wit her great grandmother comin' from church, I don't care. We gonna thump."

"Let dat shit ride," Goldie said. "It's not dat serious. Dat bitch ain't even worth all da drama."

Kat shot Goldie a venomous look. "Goldie, who da fuck side iz you on? Minez or theirz? You 'pose to rock wit me on whateva I decide to do. Fuck dat peacemaker shit! . . . I ain't lettin' shit slide! Dem dirty bitches ain't gonna jump me and get away wit it. Oh, hell, no! They want trouble, now they got it . . ."

". . . And what da fuck you call yaself doin' tanite?" Kat questioned her. "Throwin' those li'l weak-ass punches. You shoulda wilded out and grabbed a chair or somethin', and wore somebody's ass out. You see what Tender did!"

"Look how small she iz," Tender said in defense of Goldie. "She could only do so much against those big bitches."

"Yeah, you gotta point there," Kat conceded. "But I'm sayin'—"

"It's all good! Nobody got hurt, Tender interrupted. And like one a my home girls use ta say, sometimes you gotta run, run, run away, live ta fight another day. . . ."

"Umm, huh. I hear whatcha sayin'," Kat replied. "Dat shit sound good. But I'ma soldier. I grew up rumblin'. I can't do too much runnin' or takin' els. I'ma win by all means necessary. I don't care if I gotta scratch a bitch eyes out or bite her fuckin' nose off. Kat gotta come out on top. . . . I'm tryin' ta tell Mrs. Softee here to go all out too. Size don't matter. It ain't the size of da dog in da fight. It's the size of da fight in da dog."

"Well, next time," Goldie began, lying, "I'll remember that and try my best ta hurt somethin'."

"Next time? . . ." Kat said. "Fa ya sake, betta not be no next time."

Then Tender got up and stretched, signaling her sleepiness. She had seen and heard enough drama for the day.

". . . You musta read my mind." Kat sat up in her chair. "I'm tired as fuck!"

"Me, too!" Goldie added.

"I'm outta here," Kat said. "Tamorrow . . ."

When she was out of earshot, Goldie burst out laughing. "Ah, haa! Dat bitch got her ass kicked! Good fa her! . . ."

Tender stared at her, "Yo, what's so funny?" she asked. "Any one of us could have been hurt."

"Naw . . . Naw . . . Tender, I ain't laughin' at you," Goldie explained between chuckles. "It's Kat. She finally got what wuz comin' ta her. . . ."

So now Tender knew the resistance she felt while she pulled Goldie wasn't her imagination. What's really up between these two?

". . . If Kat and a grizzly bear were fightin', I'd help the bear," Goldie said. "Tender, Kat be doin' some real foul shit! I've been around her long enuff ta know . . . Yo, it's hard cheerin' fa da bad guy. I can't condone her shit forever. I seen enuff and had enuff . . . Tender, you jus' don't know . . ."

"I thought she wuz ya friend," Tender said.

Goldie replied straight-faced. "Wit friends like dat, who needs enemies."

Goldie had nothing but love for Tender. Over the few short months they had been together, they had become quite close. Tender was nice and quiet. She had the kind of humble personality that people couldn't help but like. But she would never place complete trust in another human being again. She now reserved that type of trust for her diary and God.

"Listen, Tender, ya probably think I'm wrong or just real foul, but one day you'll see fa yaself. Everything I'm tellin' you iz da truth. I ain't gotta kick dirt on nobody's name," she assured her.

By now, Tender was used to Goldie talking in riddles. She just let it go, like water under a bridge. She figured whenever Goldie was ready to totally come clean, she would. Until then she would keep her eyes open and mouth shut.

"Good night," Tender said, excusing herself from any further conversation.

"Later," Goldie simply replied.

Tender knew it would be a few more minutes before Goldie's night light went out. She watched her as she went into her nightstand drawer and pulled out her diary. Tender thought, What could be so important that she had to document it daily? Wasn't she a little too old for that?

# 6

THE CHEROKEE STRIP CLUB was a loud and blurry scene. The DJ cranked out nothing but hit music. Songs that made the strippers want to shake what their mommas gave them. They aroused the customers and the customers spent big money.

Tender was soon a featured dancer. Club owners now paid her big time to take the stage. Her dancing was hot, her moves seductive and her looks fine. Add that to her newness and innocence and you understood her popularity.

She was standing on her two feet for the first time ever. She had food, clothing and shelter. Tender was still dancing in Kat's shadow, though. Point-blank, Kat provided the shelter, was her boss and still the shit. But Tender was making a name and money for herself. As time went by, tricks, pimps and other strippers began to take notice of Kat's newest protégée . . . She worked hard, stripping every chance she got. She had visions of accumulating and saving large sums of money. She was ambitious and no longer in awe of the countless naked, half-naked and scantily clad girls who pranced around the club with abandon. Now she was just as comfortable being seen in her birthday suit as they were in theirs. The wall, lap dances and VIP treatments had become commonplace for her. She didn't even bat an eye at some of the vulgar sex acts she'd seen performed, like girls having sex with customers when they were just supposed to be lap dancing; or the perverted customers who masturbated in full view. In the back of her mind, she understood that one day, she too would be participating in some of these same acts if she wanted to make major money.

Tender squatted down, opened her legs, and gave up a full view of her neatly trimmed pussy. Then she began to thrust her hips and shake her titties. Getting down on all fours, with her back slightly arched, she began slapping her own baby oil–coated ass cheeks.

The customers responded by crowding the stage, touching her ass, while they showered her with dollars. Some even took it a step further, sticking their fingers inside her. Tender tried to be cool but it was hard. She often wondered where their fingers had been before they touched her.

"Give it up fa my girl Tender," the DJ said, as she gathered up her belongings and her money.

As she made her way back to the dressing room, guys continued to harass and proposition her, making nasty comments about what they wanted to do to her. Tender ignored them all. She smiled and kept it moving. She was more concerned with counting her money and washing up. There was something about stripping that made her feel nasty.

"Go Tender! Go Tender! . . ." Kat began to chant, after following her into the dressing room. ". . . Ain't a bitch in dis club got shit on you. Except fa me."

"Don't I know it!" she laughed. "It's ya world and I'm jus' a squirrel tryin' ta get a nut."

"Whateva!" Kat joked. "Listen, dis nigga out there tryin' ta holla at you 'bout somethin'?"

"'Bout what?" she asked, as she put her foot on a chair and began to wipe her private parts with baby wipes.

"Stop playin' stupid," Kat replied. "C'mon, you know what it's about? A VIP. You know where da 'real' dough at . . . Don't front, we already talked about dis. If you wanna make major paper in here, dis is what you gotta do. Da shit iz easy money. . . ."

Kat had been trying to get her to do VIPs for a while. Certain men came to the club thinking—Why pay for just a dance when you can have sex? For a little more money, they could get the whole thing—total sex.

She had had enough of that when she lived in the street. She wasn't trying to go back to doing just anything. But she did want the big money, so she could get out of the game sooner than later.

Before they could get another word out their mouths, Goldie walked in.

"What's goin' on here? My clique havin' a meetin' witout me?" she said.

"Nah, I'm jus' tryin' ta get Ms. Goody Two Shoes here ta VIP . . . Would you tell her that's what's up," Kat stated.

Oblivious to Tender, who was busy cleaning herself up, Kat shot Goldie "the eye." Along with a few facial expressions that said, "You better help me talk her into this."

"Yo, Tender," Goldie spoke up reluctantly, with faked enthusiasm, "get dat dough Ma . . . It'll be over before you know it. Wham, bam, thank you ma'am. These niggas iz minute men. They ain't tryin' ta make love, they tryin' ta bust a nut . . . Tender, you gotta step up ya game! Da money's out there, waitin'." She pulled Tender's coat to the prices for various sex acts. "Go get it!"

Goldie gave Tender the confidence she needed. There was something reassuring in her voice that just made Tender want to believe every word she said.

"Okay," Tender finally agreed, as she stepped into a thong, "let's do dis. Where he at?"

"That's what's up!" Kat exclaimed happily. "You 'bout it, 'bout it! . . . C'mon, now let me show you dis nigga."

Tender followed Kat out the dressing room and back into the club. As she did she turned around and gave Goldie a look that said "Here goes nothin'. I'm goin' all out."

Goldie gave Tender a hollow smile, and she felt terrible that she had allowed herself to be used by Kat to suck someone in again. She genuinely liked Tender. And she didn't want to see her turned out or burned out like so many other girls in the club—on cocaine, heroin and Ecstasy—being pimped hard. She didn't want to see Tender get in the game deeper and make a bad situation worse, just like she had.

As soon as they left, Goldie got up and walked out behind them. She needed some liquor in her system. To ease her guilty conscience.

"Whitey," Kat began her introduction, "dis my peepz, Tender. Tender, dis my nigga, Whitey. Now that ya'll been introduced, handle ya bizness." With that said, Kat turned and walked away. She was confident that her pupil would follow the game plan to a tee.

"What's poppin', shorty?" He greeted her with a big Kool-Aid smile.

"It's whateva, wit me!" she shot back.

The first thing she noticed about the guy in front of her was that he was ugly. There was no getting around that. He was light, bright and damn near white, as they say. This explained his name. One thing Tender couldn't tolerate more than an ugly dark-skinned guy, was an ugly light-skinned guy. It was somehow acceptable in her book though to be ugly and dark. Those two images were embedded in her subconscious from day one by

white society. At one time or another, she had heard, "you ugly
black motherfucker," this and that. But to her, to be ugly and
light-skinned was definitely a curse from God. His nose was big.
And his nostrils were wide. It made him slightly resemble a pig.
That was a major turnoff to her.

But whatever Whitey lacked in the looks department, he
more than made up for in the pockets. He was getting major
paper hustling in South Philly's Tasker projects. He was immacu-
lately dressed in a crushed black linen suit, with matching black
gators. A long platinum chain, with a scorpion medallion encrusted in diamonds, rested near his navel. This attention grab-
ber highlighted his whole outfit.

"How much?" he suddenly asked, getting right to the point.
He recklessly eyeballed her body.

"Huh? . . ." Tender exclaimed, taken aback by his directness.
". . . I mean, it depends on what you tryin' ta get into, playboy . . ."

"Well, I want it all! Gimme da whole package!" he replied
nastily.

"Well, you've got da wrong chick. I don't do it all. Ain't nobody
fuckin' me in da ass! I don't rock like dat . . ." she insisted. "Now,
I'll fuck you or give some head. But anything other than that, you
gotta holla at somebody else. 'Cause I ain't wit it . . ."

Yeah, right! That's what they all say. Whitey thought. He knew
from previous experiences that almost every stripper could be
bought for a price. The higher the pay, the lower they'd stoop. No
doubt about it.

Tender continued, ". . . I charge three hundred dollars an
hour for a date. But since dis ain't a official date, I'll give you a
break. Gimme a hundred dollars fa head or a buck fifty for a shot
of cock. Two hundred fa both."

"C'mon," Whitey said, as he led the way to the VIP room.

Money wasn't an issue to him, he was just asking the price just to be asking. He paid for what he wanted, especially when it came to sex. And tonight was no exception; he was feeling horny.

The VIP room was a small dimly lit room, less than half the size of a studio apartment, with bland dirty-white walls. There was nothing more inside than a large well-worn black leather couch. It also served as a bed.

Once inside the room, Whitey whipped out a large knot of money. It was the likes of which Tender had never seen before in her life. He peeled off three hundred-dollar bills and handed them to her. As if to say, "You ain't doin' me no favors."

"Now, let's do the damn thing!" he demanded. "I want da best of both worlds."

Tender took the money and put it into her ever present clutch bag that she carried. Suddenly, she began to have second thoughts. But she had committed herself now—there was no turning back.

Going back into her bag, Tender pulled out a condom and some spermicidal jelly. She also used it as a lubricant. Quickly, she tried to don him with the condom. But he balked.

"Dig dis here," he said. "I don't like gettin' my dick sucked wit no rubber on. I can't feel it."

"Listen," Tender began. "I ain't goin' raw dog wit nobody! I ain't sayin' you got somethin'. But at da same time I ain't tryin' ta catch nuttin' either . . . Da rubber iz fa both our protection."

"I'ma put da rubber on," he said forcefully. "Jus' hit me off wit some brains, first. Already told you them shits don't do me no justice."

Hearing the anger in his voice, Tender's heart raced. Her fear and inexperience made her cave into his demands. She did as she was told.

Laid back on the couch, Whitey watched as she went down on him. Slowly, she inspected his uncircumcised dick for any bumps, dirt or irregularities. Finding none, she put it in her mouth, and gently began sucking on it, till it was fully erect. As she did so, Tender let large globs of saliva run out her mouth onto his member. Up and down she went licking and jerking his dick simultaneously, while a pleased Whitey just tilted his head and closed his eyes, enjoying the sensation. Then suddenly right in the middle of it, Tender stopped. Visibly pissed, on the verge of cuming, he wondered what was wrong.

"Why you stop?" he demanded to know.

With his dick gripped tightly in one hand, Tender pulled her mouth off his manhood, inspecting it again. Then with her free hand, she went inside her mouth and removed a follicle of hair.

"Somethin wuz in my mouth," she replied, as she spat lightly toward the floor. She tried to remove any other foreign object that may also have been in there.

For a few more minutes, she sucked him off furiously. She always stopped just before he came. She took him to the edge of ecstasy, constantly frustrating him.

Now that Whitey was fully aroused, he wanted to fuck. He wanted to give it to her hard and fast. He wanted to be in control. "That's enuff!" he stated. "What da pussy do? Let's see if you can take da dick . . ."

As they flip-flopped positions, Tender slid out of her thong. She assumed a missionary position while Whitey put on a condom, as promised. He had to, he had a girl at home. He couldn't afford to bring a disease back to her. That was the last thing he needed. God forbid, he would never hear the end of it.

"Umm . . ." He moaned as he slipped inside of her. He couldn't believe how warm and tight she was. This was some good young pussy, he thought. After a few long strokes, he really got into it, trying to kiss on Tender. To which she responded by just turning her head. She wanted no part of that.

Tender all but froze underneath him. Her mind left her body

and went back to that ugly moment when her mother's boyfriend raped her. She felt sick and began to gulp air in an attempt to catch her breath and calm her senses. Whitey thought she was getting off on him. "Yeah baby. I'm hittin' it."

He bent her legs behind her head, and pounded away, like a battering ram at Tender's pussy. "Aaarrghh!" he grunted loudly as he climaxed. Losing his composure, he collapsed on top of her.

She wanted to cry but she kept her composure. She was relieved that he finally came. Now she had to get him up off of her. "Get up! I can't breathe!" she commanded him.

Drained, Whitey slowly complied. Standing over her, he began to get himself together. And she did likewise. But before he departed he offered her a small piece of advice.

"Not fa nuttin'," he explained. "Listen, if dis iz how you eatin' . . ." He looked her in the eye. "VIPing, dating and dancing, you gotta be more into the things you do. Or don't do 'em. You act like you didn't wanna be here or somethin'. Dat was a half-ass fuck. Yeah, I came cause da pussy wuz proper. But it coulda been betta you put a li'l emotion into it. Fake it if you have to, wit dat bomb-ass shot of cock you got, a nigga'll give anything. I know, I've been out there like dat before . . . I done had all the hos up in dis joint twice, and none of 'em got nuttin' on dat pussy you got. You jus' gotta." He had his clothes back on now.

"Faget it, I told you enuff already." Tender was no dummy; she didn't take offense to what he was saying. On the contrary, she was paying attention.

Tender, Goldie and Kat went on a shopping spree at the Galleria mall in downtown Philly. In and out of some of the trendiest fashion boutiques, the trio strolled in like the three musketeers, purchasing whatever their hearts desired.

Tender was now making close to fifteen hundred dollars a week—this was the kind of money every stripper could only hope for. She had never seen that type of money before. A fool with money was a terrible thing. She knew she had to be smart. So secretly, she opened up her own bank account as well as keeping a stash around the house.

Unlike so many strippers who had been dancing for months, even years, and had nothing to show for it, Tender had a plan—she was going to be an entrepreneur. She figured if she failed to plan, then she had better plan to fail. The clothes were an investment in herself. Clothes enhanced one's looks and status. It increased one's appeal and earning ability. It was simple, the better she looked, the more desirable she was. The more tricks/dates she could do, the more money she could make.

They spent thousands apiece on Gucci frames, Marc Jacobs and Kate Spade bags, Prada and Dolce & Gabana shoes and Frankie B jeans. You name it, they bought it. Since neither Goldie nor Tender knew too much about expensive clothes, being fly to them consisted of a tight pair of jeans, football or basketball jersey and a fitted hat. Kat acted as their fashion consultant though, approving or disapproving of their every purchase.

Personally, Kat would rather look like a million and not have a dollar in her pocket, than dress or live below her standards and have a ton of money in the bank. Luckily for her, she somehow managed to maintain a happy medium. She enjoyed the best of both worlds.

She didn't like anybody copycatting her style. It was cool for her clique to buy the same designers she had, just as long as it was a different color or style. She didn't want to be seen in the streets looking like the Bobbsey twins. That wasn't cool in her book. But in the back of her mind she knew they wouldn't be able to hook it up like her. She was teaching them everything they knew, not everything that she knew.

Tender spent about two thousand dollars that day alone and she didn't even blink. The money was coming like that and there was more where that came from.

"Damn, Tender!" Kat exclaimed, as they ate dinner at the trendy Houston's restaurant, "you gone be shittin' on bitches. You got lotsa outfits. Fly shit too! . . ."

"I know, right!" Tender agreed. She took the compliment in stride. She was like a modern-day Cinderella.

"Now don't be throwin' ya new stuff in da washer machine!" Goldie said jokingly. "This ain't that hood wear. These fabrics iz delicate. So handle with care. Send them to the cleaners . . ."

"Stop playin'!" Tender countered, while chewing on a piece of steak. "I'ma take care of my things. Trust me, when you neva had nuttin', you treasure everything . . ."

"Clothes ain't nuttin'. You can get whateva you want if you focus. You just gotta be willin' ta do whateva. Know no limits."

# 7

"G LORIA," her mother whispered gently, as she lovingly brushed her hair in preparation for school. "I have something for you."

"What, Ma?"

"Just close your eyes and I'll give it to you." Ms. Cruz reached into the pocket of her housedress.

"Okay, open your eyes."

Ms. Cruz removed a 24K gold, herringbone chain with a matching crucifix. "Oh, Mama, thank you! It's beautiful. This is a gift for doing well in school?"

"Give it to me. Let me put it around your neck," her mother said. She fastened the clasp. "Mama, I love it. I'm never gonna take it off. Not even when I'm married . . ."

"Gloria, one day you are going to make some man very happy," her mother promised. "You'll be a gorgeous bride. Watch! . . . Just always remember what I tell you. Books . . ."

". . . No boys!" Gloria said, finishing her mother's sentence. She heard it all before, at least a million times. So much so, she was sick of it. She knew her mother was only trying to protect her and guide her right.

But young Gloria also knew that something else motivated her overprotective thing. Her mother had a thing against boys. She never had anything good to say about them. But how bad could men be? she often thought. After all, she wouldn't be here in this world without one.

Goldie often dreamed about this and other happier times in her life. This was her way to escape the present reality. Her mind trips, more often than not, also often took a turn for the worse. They took her back to the bad moments as well, bringing back the pain and tears.

She tossed and turned on her bed.

". . . No, Mami! No!" She threw her hands up to block an imaginary blow.

The room was moonlit enough that Tender could see the commotion from a few feet away. These screaming episodes and bad dreams she'd seen before. It had been occasional but they were becoming more and more frequent. Gloria was waking up from nightmares so often these days that it was beginning to affect Tender's own sleeping pattern. Kat was a heavy sleeper, though, and on top of that she slept way down the hall. So she missed the drama.

Tender knew better than to wake a sleeping person up out of a bad dream. So she patiently watched and waited until Goldie had calmed down a bit. Tender walked over to her bed and gently whispered her name. "Goldie . . . Goldie," she whispered. "Girl, you alright?"

Hearing her stripper name brought Goldie back into reality and out of her dream.

"Huh? . . ." She pried open her eyes, straining to focus on the figure in front of her. "What time is it? It ain't mornin' yet, is it?"

"Naw," Tender answered. "What'z up wit you? You wuz callin'

out in ya sleep again! Screamin' and carryin' on . . . Musta been some dream, huh?"

ANOTHER NIGHT, another dollar for Tender, Kat and Goldie. They were back at the club, chasing paper. Kat sat at the bar drinking Hennessy straight—in no apparent hurry—since she had already gone out on a few dates, while Tender dressed. Goldie, on the other hand, was busy VIPing with a regular customer of hers.

Coming out of the dressing room, Tender was approached by Jules, a local pimp, who frequented the clubs to check up on his hos and seek out new "stock." Jules was light-skinned, average height, medium build with curly black hair. He was a self-proclaimed pretty boy with the gift of gab. When angered, his temper was legendary.

"Hey Tenda! Tenda!" he called out, as he motioned with his hand for her to come here. "Lemme holla atcha' fa a minute. Just a moment of ya time, if you would be so kind."

Warning bells went off in her head. She knew who he was and what he was about. Kat and Goldie had pointed him out on several occasions and warned her to stay away from him. They said he was, most notably, Cookie's pimp.

"Dig, Tender," he began. "I've been checkin' you out fa months now. And I'm really diggin' ya style. You ain't like da average broad around here. I like da way you carry yaself. Na'mean? Ya real low key. But what I respect most about you iz da way you grind. Real recognize real. I see you got da makin's of a star. You just need da proper guidance, direction . . ."

He scanned every inch of her tight young body. She thought she was used to this kind of thing by now but he was making her feel uneasy.

"Michael Jordan didn't start winnin' championships till the right coach came on board. And that's what I am, that's what I do.

I'm da coach. I point you in the right direction. Listen, sweetheart, you got superstar written all over you. But you ain't neva gonna make it to da big dance witout me . . . All dat glitters ain't gold. You fuckin' wit da wrong people at da right time. You wastin' ya potential hon, fuckin' wit these rinky-dink clubs and lame-ass niggas. I could hook you up wit my escort service or massage parlor downtown that only caters to rich crackers. They'd love ya ta death. You'd make a muthafuckin' killin' . . . Wit ya beauty and my brains we'd . . ."

Tender stared blankly at Jules, thinking he didn't look like a pimp. Well, he didn't look like any pimp she'd ever seen on TV. They had flashy clothes, big hats and women hanging all over them. Those days were long gone, replaced by a new breed of wannabe pimps and baby macks.

Jules continued, beating Tender in the head with his bullshit. "You like money, right, Tender? Yeah, I know you do! I can tell by da fly-ass clothes dat you be wearin' . . . But iz you ready ta go all out? Ta take ya game to da next level, you gotta be ready ta do da damn thing. I'm talkin' car money, house money. Fuck a mink and those clothes! They go in and outta style. I'm talkin' about purchasing things dat hold some weight in dis world . . . I know you VIPing and e'rything. If da price is right, you'll fuck a nigga all night. Feel me now, Tender, you up in here shakin' ya ass, niggas feelin' on you. Sometimes fa free or givin' you whateva he wants to, a dolla or two. A lousy fuckin' single! Now tell me, what da fuck is a dolla ta a queen like you? Na'mean. Tenda, if you roll wit a nigga like me, I promise you, we gone eat fa real."

Tender gave him a "Nigga, Please! Save your breath" look. She wasn't the least bit moved by what he had been saying. Tender may have been young and new to the game, but she was far from dumb.

". . . So whatcha say?" Jules asked confidently, ignoring the look that was plastered on her face. "You wit me or what? Girl, what I'm tryin' ta say iz, lemme help you help yaself. . . ."

Jules was thinking that Kat was probably the only thing standing in the way of him copping Tender. If she hadn't brainwashed or pulled her coat to his game then he had as good a shot as any pimp in the club of pulling her into his stable. It might break his back, it might make him cry, but nothing beats a failure except a try, he always told himself.

Tender sucked her teeth. "I can't fuck wit you like dat," she said. "I'm good! . . . Now excuse me, I gotta go make my money."

Jules thought he had laid his mack down. She took him by surprise.

"You li'l nappy-head, bum-bitch! Dig dis here, I'm tryin' ta help *you* out. Bitch, you can't help me or hurt me," he barked. "Ho, fa e'ryone of ya dat say no, a dozen of ya say yes. One monkey don't stop no show! Bitch, dis Jules! I do what I do! . . . I shoulda known betta dan ta fuck wit ya renegade-affiliated ass. You, Kat and Goldie can eat a dick, fa all I care . . . Anyway, you might as well let me pimp you, cause Kat gonna do it anyway. Yo, I swear ta God I'ma hurt one a you sluts one day . . ."

Yeah, yeah, yeah! Tender thought. Most dudes couldn't handle rejection well, and Jules was definitely one of them. But Jules also didn't make idle threats.

Tender walked away from him. He could disrespect her verbally all he wanted to, just as long as he didn't put his hands on her.

There was work to do and money to be made and she didn't need a pimp to do it. She stepped right to her business. Spotting a regular customer, she moved right up on him.

"What'z up, Daddy?" she said seductively, trying to stroke his ego. "I missed you. Where you been? Lemme find out—you cheatin' on me?"

Tender was good about talking to her customers and even gave them good advice. Guys felt at ease and let down their guard with her. She gave them special attention and everything else they didn't get at home—eagerly, they gave up that cash—before, during and after.

Tender got him to buy her an overpriced drink at the bar, which she let just sit in front of her. She needed to fulfill her drink minimum. Somehow, though, as they continued to talk, she rubbed his thigh and managed to brush her breasts up against him numerous times.

"So what'z it gonna be tanite, Daddy? You watchin' or you participatin'?"

A sly smile quickly spread across his face. That told her what time it was. He was ready to make that move to the VIP room. Tender gently grabbed his hand and led him there.

After he handed her the money, Tender reached into her black Gucci clutch bag and grabbed a condom.

She placed the condom on his penis and assumed a position between his legs. She knew just what he liked. She sucked on his penis like life depended on it, keeping her eyes locked in on his the whole time. Her eyes said, "cum for me. Bust a nut in my mouth, Daddy." He came back to Tender time and time again, just for this.

Tender sucked, spat and licked on his penis, making loud nasty slurping sounds. This drove him wild. She went the extra mile to please her people. She gave service with a smile.

Running her tongue underneath his penis, Tender licked till she reached his balls. Then she inserted them into her mouth and began to hum on them. This drove him bananas. She gripped his penis tightly as if she were choking the dear life out of it, as she jerked him off. In a matter of seconds he delivered a condom full of cum.

"OOOOoohhhh!"

Tender smiled, knowing that he'd be back to give her more money real soon. Climbing to her feet, she removed the slimy condom from his penis, while he lay on the couch trying to savor the moment.

"Aiight, Daddy, we gotta go. Other people gotta use this room," she explained, while sending him on his way. "Don't be no stranger. Come thru and holla more often . . ."

"No doubt! You know I gotta thing fa you. You maka nigga wanna leave home. Fa real." He actually always ended up feeling like a cold-blooded sucker for paying for head. Especially with someone who would only be his for the moment. The minute he came or ran out of money, she was gone. She moved on to the next man. It was nothing personal, strictly business. He had to have it, but hated having it.

Tender blazed a trail to the VIP room and the club. She served customer after customer, making money on top of money. These tricks were just a faceless and nameless bunch to her. A way out of the bad situation.

Tender was at the bar nursing a ginger ale, while Kat downed one apple martini after another and Goldie drank shots of Hennessy.

"I'm tellin' y'all, dat nigga wuz tight!" Tender said, referring to Jules. "He came all out his face, sayin' if we fuck wit any of his hos again, he was gonna see us. Handle his bizness and shit . . ."

Kat chuckled, "Fuck 'im! He ain't no threat. Don't let 'im scare you. Muthafuckin' po' pimp dat's been listenin' to too many Too Short albums . . . I wish he would even look like he wanna move out against us. I know some wild gung ho niggas from North Philly that'll tear his ass out da frame. All it takes is one phone call. And it'll be about his ASS! He talk dat gangsta seventies pimp shit, but fa real, fa real he don't want it . . ."

That's comforting to know, thought Tender. At least they had some backup if Jules tried to make good on his threats. Or if anything else should go wrong in the club, Kat had thugs on the team.

Goldie sat back listening to Kat's boasts. As long as she'd known Kat, she'd never actually seen her legendary gang. But she sure heard plenty about them. All that tough talk from Kat went in one ear and out the other.

". . . Dat nigga iz all mouth," she continued. "He still mad about da way we whipped up on his hos. And now dat you dissed him, he really tight. So he gonna hide behind dat. But I ain't stupid, I know why he really mad. Feel me. His bitches took an 'L'."

"Yeah, dat nigga definitely on some ole extra shit," Tender added. "Homo-thug, he wanna talk shit ta me. Cause I'ma fuckin' female."

Kat stated, "Jules think his game iz so tight. Only because he be pullin' 'em dumb, young, and weak-minded hos. He gets them, now he feel he can pull e'rybody. . . ."

As they talked, unbeknownst to them someone was approaching them from behind. The light tap on the shoulder startled Tender. Her heart almost stopped; she thought it was Jules.

"Tonya, Tonya Morris," the man said.

At that point, Tender knew that this couldn't have been Jules. He didn't know her real name. She herself had almost forgotten her government name, she hadn't heard it in so long.

As she spun around on the bar stool, "What up, cuz?" the young man asked, with a wide grin on his face. "Long time no see! So dis iz whatcha been up to? Huh? . . . Dig, don't worry 'bout me, I can keep a secret. Just hit me off wit a couple dollars e'ry now and then. And I ain't seen you. Feel me? I mean you are a li'l too young to even be up in dis spot. Somebody could get in some *serious trouble*, fuckin' wit you . . ."

The blood in Tender's veins began to boil. It was her second cousin, Terrence. He was one of the principal reasons she ran away from her so-called family. He was one of the men in the family who tried to sexually assault her. Not even time could quell her anger.

So here she was, half-naked and full of rage, as he stood over her grinning, with lust in his eyes. He was probably replaying all those nights he had attempted to have his way with her.

Goldie interrupted their stare-down. "Tender, who dis nigga callin' you by ya handle like dat?"

"Nobody!" Tender replied through clenched teeth.

"Oh, I'm nobody now?" the man said. "Keep treatin' me like a stepchild and the cost of livin' iz gonna go up. You betta be nice ta me, if you know what's good for you."

Cocky, her cousin took a step forward, ignoring Kat and Goldie, and tried to pull Tender aside for a long talk. He thought he could use some scare tactics on her once they were alone. But this wasn't the same Tonya he knew. This wasn't the same timid kid that stepped up in the club a few months ago. No, that Tonya was gone forever, just like the innocence she once possessed.

Tender quickly pushed him away, shoving him hard in the chest. "Get ya fuckin' hands off me! You bitch-ass nigga!"

Finding that funny, he advanced toward her again. Only this time he was met with resistance. Tender grabbed her drinking glass and cracked him upside the head with it, stunning him long enough for her friends to jump on him and pound him out. Instantly, the ruckus caught the attention of the big beefy bouncers. They rushed over and subdued the man before any other acts of violence could take place.

"Lemme go!" he hollered, as they dragged him out the club. "I didn't touch them bitches. They hit *me!*"

Treating him as if he were a drunk, a jealous boyfriend or psycho customer, they roughed him up, disregarding everything he had to say. It was as if he were telling a lie. The bouncers had seen and heard it all before. That was one thing about working in a club that served alcohol; after a few drinks the liquor brought out the worst in people. Even nice guys became unruly.

". . . I'm callin' da cops!" he threatened. "Y'all got unda age girlz up in here . . ."

Many of the club's loyal customers took offense to his last comment. They couldn't bear to think about their favorite strip joint getting shut down. So they went outside to straighten him out.

Just when Tender thought she had put her family out of her mind, life had thrown a reminder in her face.

"Yo, wuz dat nigga really ya cousin?" Kat questioned her. "Dat nigga wuz trippin' fa real!"

"Uh-huh," Tender responded. "He ain't nuttin' but a tree jumper! A baby raper!"

That's heavy, Kat thought. Now she was mad that they didn't do some real damage to him.

"And dat's 'pose ta be ya cousin?" Goldie commented. "Dat nigga oughta be shot."

Tender went on explaining the nasty details of her ordeal at her family's house. ". . . Yo, you got e'ry reason in da world ta stay away from dem rotten muthafuckas," Kat insisted. "They ain't ya family! Me and Goldie iz ya new family now."

Tender felt warm inside. She did have two people in her corner. At least that's what she thought.

# 8

T HE LOOK ON KAT'S FACE said it all. Her eyes were squinting and her jaw and mouth were tighter than a closed fist. As soon as Tender and Goldie laid eyes on her, they saw evil and knew it was trouble, with a capital T.

"Yo, I took my eye off my clutch bag while I was dancing and one a these petty-ass bitches went into my bag and stole my locker key. I go back to the locker room ta freshen up and when I open up my locker my shit was all fucked up. I ain't stupid now, I know how I left my shit. First thing I do is look fa my paper and dat shit was gone . . . Three hundred fuckin' dollars gone! I ain't neva been robbed in my life and I ain't gonna let it start now. Matter fact, they didn't even rob me, they stole from me. Sneak-thiefed me! Somebody gonna get it! . . ." Kat announced. Animated, she kept moving her hands while she talked.

"Do you know who did it?" Tender asked innocently, a logical question.

"Yeah, I know who did it!" she barked. "Fuckin' Cookie and 'em! Somebody told me they seen her creepin' out da locker room 'round da time I was up on stage . . . I'm tired of her shit. C'mon, I'm searchin' lockers. Da first bitch dat buck, we gonna move out on her."

Goldie thought, Here comes the B.S. again. She'd been around Kat so long she knew when she was telling the truth. And right now she knew Kat was lying through her teeth. But Cookie was a prime suspect. Kat singled Cookie out because she was at the top of her shit list. Goldie had had a serious buzz going on and Kat just blew it with all this drama.

As they went to the locker room in search of Cookie, Goldie caught a bad vibe. Over the years, Goldie had developed a sixth sense for trouble from working in the clubs and surviving on the streets. Something bad was about to go down. She knew it, but she couldn't put her finger on it.

Cookie was up on stage and easy to get to, but Kat decided against causing a scene. Instead, she concocted a plan to ambush her when she came back to the locker room. Tender, Kat and Goldie got ready to rumble. They changed into their street clothes, pulled their hair back into ponytails, and greased their faces with Vaseline to protect against scratches. Kat then instructed everybody to take the locks off their lockers and put them into a sock, which is commonly referred to in prison as a lock-in-a-sock.

Wrapping the weapons tightly around their hands, Kat, Goldie and Tender lay in wait for their would-be victim.

Cookie headed back toward the locker room to freshen up. She had danced on stage for a half hour straight and VIPed with a customer. Her home girls weren't around. Some of them were doing a private party and the others were out on dates. The money must have been good because they hadn't shown up yet, on a Friday night at that.

There would be hell to pay if she didn't make Jules's quota for the night. He'd probably beat her ass and then take her down-town to center city to walk the track, if she didn't come correct. So she had to freshen up and get right back on her paper chase.

Pressed tightly up against the wall, Kat, Goldie and Tender concealed themselves. The locker room appeared empty to Cookie at first. She walked straight into their trap. Kat pounced on her from the blind side, swinging the lock-in-a-sock, striking Cookie on the side of the head. It happened so fast she never saw it coming.

"Aaaaww!" she managed to say, before crumpling to the floor holding her head.

"Bitch, you like stealin', huh?" Kat asked. As Cookie curled up into a fetal position to protect herself and took the beat down, she had no other choice. The lock-in-a-sock made a sickening thud sound each time it found it's mark.

"Why are you doin' this ta me?" she begged.

"Shut up, ho! Take dis ass-whuppin' like da man you iz . . . Dis oughta teach ya ass a lesson 'bout takin' stuff dat don't belong ta ya," Kat spat.

Kat continued to swing her weapon but the other girls began to feel sorry for Cookie. Enough was enough. Kat was going over-board. This had the makings of a murder written all over it and Tender and Goldie wanted no part of that.

Tender finally worked up enough nerve to pull Kat off the girl. "Stop it! Dat's enough!" she insisted. "We gotta get outta here."

After Tender wrestled Kat away from her, Goldie stood in a daze over Cookie, amazed at all the bodily harm that they had caused. Cookie was bloody and almost motionless. The low sick moans that escaped her body were the only signs of life. She had lumps and bumps all over her body. The knots on her head looked grotesque. The sight of her face sent a chill down Goldie's spine.

With Kat still fuming and Goldie going into shock, Tender took control of the situation. "C'mon, y'all," she ordered. "Grab ya shit, we out!"

Quickly, they all tipped out and exited the club. They left Cookie to be discovered by another dancer.

Inside Kat's truck, they breathed a sigh of relief. They pulled away from the club and headed for home.

No one said a word while they drove. Each one of them was alone with their thoughts. They were alone to contemplate their actions. Kat, for one, didn't feel any remorse whatsoever. She lived by her motto, "If it ain't rough, it ain't right." In her mind she just got even and did Cookie dirtier than they did her. Turnabout was fair play, in Kat's book.

Tender sat in the passenger seat, unable to concentrate on the *Scarface* movie on the DVD in the truck. She stared out the tinted window, watching the road. She hoped nothing was seriously wrong with Cookie, for all their sakes. After all, the dispute was pretty petty. It wasn't worth dying or going to jail over.

Meanwhile Goldie sat in the backseat fretting to herself. This was all Kat's fault, she thought. She cursed the day she met her.

"What?" Jules barked into his cell phone. "They did what? . . . I dun told 'em hos 'bout fuckin' wit mine . . . Naw, fuck dat! Them bitches violated me for the last time. On e'rything I love, I'ma murda them hos. They got my bottom bitch all laid up in da hospital . . .."

Jules was furious; he felt like not only did Kat, Goldie and Tender disrespect him, but now they took food out of his mouth. They injured one of his top hos and best moneymakers. They challenged his manhood. What kind of pimp would he be if he let a bunch of renegades run through his stable without any repercussions. He had to set an example.

•  •  •

THE OWNER OF THE CLUB banned Kat, Goldie and Tender from working there again. They really didn't care though. Strip joints were almost as plentiful as drugs and liquor stores in the hood. There were plenty of other hole-in-the-wall clubs that would gladly hire them.

The girls kept a low profile until they found out Cookie was alright. Then they bounced around from club to club, even journeying outside of Philly to Trenton, New Jersey. They felt pretty confident that Cookie wouldn't go to the police. Cookie was from the street like they were. She knew the code.

Cookie took her beat down like a champ and didn't tell, but it wasn't her who the girls should have been worried about. Jules already put the word out among his people that he wanted to see them.

Tender counted her money ". . . four hundred, five hundred, six hundred . . ." as she got dressed to go home.

Tonight was a good night at the Grindstone; it was the weekend.

Kat watched Tender like a hawk from nearby. She had a knot of money of her own, but she had a bad habit of counting other people's money too. Tender was giving her rent and utilities money but Kat wanted more. She just had to figure out a way to finesse Tender out of it.

"Yo, Tender, whatcha doin' wit all ya dough, besides buyin' clothes?" she questioned.

"I'm savin' it!" Tender quickly replied. "I'm tryin' to have somethin' ta show fa shakin' my ass. I'm not doin' dis shit fa nuttin' . . . Maybe one day I'll open up a beauty salon. You know how I like keepin' my wig tight."

"Umm, Uh! I hear ya," she replied. "You startin' ta sound more like Goldie e'ryday. Y'all bitches like what Biggie Smalls said on dat *Ready to Die* album, 'Y'all got big plans, big plans . . . ' "

Goldie smiled; she knew that Tender had not only heard her,

but was listening and taking advice. There was nothing wrong with that. Goldie wanted to be sure that Tender didn't become as financially dependent on Kat as she was.

". . . Not to be in ya business, but you really should think about investing ya money. Dat's what me and Goldie are doin'. We got our money in 401ks, money market accounts, tax shelters; our investments are diversified. We got our money making us more money. Dat's betta than stashin' ya money 'round da house or throwin' it in da bank gettin' low interest rates and payin' mad taxes on it. Jus give it ta me, trust me, I'll have you real decent in a few months."

Goldie shot Tender a look that said, "Don't do it!" But neither Tender nor Kat caught it. They were too busy talking.

Tender had always heard about the stock market. But she didn't have the slightest idea on how it worked or how to invest in it. She'd heard stories from teachers at school, how a simple investment had made people rich. Kat seemed to know what she was talking about.

"Lemme check my stash, see what I'm workin' wit. I'm gonna get back wit you on dat," she said.

"Aiight." Kat exclaimed. She couldn't wait to get her hands on Tender's money.

In the wee hours, the girls exited the club, stepping into the cool morning air. Among the last to leave, the trio walked less than half a block to Kat's truck. The white Escalade stood out like diamond, sparkling under the city lights.

The steady sound of high-heel shoes meeting the concrete could be heard on the abandoned block. Kat, Goldie and Tender were alone on these streets, or so they thought. Unbeknownst to them, a pair of eyes were watching from the shadows. Jules lay low in a hooptie across the street, a few feet in back of the truck. As the trio walked past him, he ducked down. He heard the voices of Tender and Goldie loud and clear.

". . . I don't know why you even lyin' like dat. You know I always win. I can't even remember the last time you beat me," Tender stated. They were having a friendly argument about who beat who last time in a game on PlayStation 2. "Oh, yeah!" Goldie said. "Then bet somethin'. I get serious when money's involved."

"We can bet whatever," Tender agreed. "You ain't said nuttin' . . ."

Kat pushed the automatic starter and her truck's engine purred to life. Her truck was boxed in by two other vehicles. She didn't like other cars being so close to hers—because that's how dents and scratches happen. Opening the doors, she hopped in the driver's seat while Goldie and Tender climbed in the back-seat to do battle. She let her truck warm up, gently easing her foot down on the gas . . . While she revved the engine, she blasted a classic tune by rapper Jay-Z and Foxy Brown, "Ain't no nigga like da one I got. No one can fuck you better . . ."

Meanwhile, behind them, Jules had quietly slipped out of his car. Crouched low, he crept up on the truck, gun in hand. He by-passed the passengers and went straight to the driver's window. He raised up, pointing a nine-millimeter Taurus at Kat's head.

"Open dis muthafuckin' door, bitch, befo' I blow ya fuckin' head off!" he commanded. She froze. Then her bladder gave way. She peed on herself.

"Bitch, you got two seconds to open dis before I start bangin'!" he barked again.

Fear spread through the truck like chicken pox in grammar school. Kat didn't know whether to do what he said or take her chances and try to pull off. Either way, this was a bad situation. Only God knew what he was going to do to them. Where were the cops when you really needed them?

"One . . . Two . . ." he counted as he clutched his gun. He didn't want to murder them right here without getting any money. And he didn't want to run the risk of getting caught. He hesitated.

*"BBBOOOMMM!!!"* The bullet ripped through the back window, shattering the glass. It came from inside the truck and lodged in the side of Jules's head. He crumpled to the ground instantly, never knowing who or what hit him.

Kat snapped out of her daze and threw the truck in gear. She peeled off into the night.

BACK AT THE HOUSE, Goldie sat and shook while Kat paced the living room rug. She had to figure a way out of this mess. Tender was feeling the strain too but tried not to show it the way Goldie was. She didn't want to be considered the weak link.

"Yo, listen up!" Kat suddenly spoke. "We gotta get da fuck outta here. We gotta leave Philly . . . At least till shit cools down . . ."

"Where to?" Tender asked. "Where do you have in mind?"

"Miami," Kat suggested. "Now hurry up, let's go pack!"

Tender always wanted to go to Miami. She grew up watching *Miami Vice* reruns on cable. Something about that city captured her imagination. Yet she never dreamed she'd go under these conditions.

# 9

K AT, GOLDIE AND TENDER secured last-minute reser-
vations on standby. So they had to wait around the airport
for hours. It was Memorial Day weekend and Miami was the latest hotspot where players played. Like a magnet, it attracted
thousands upon thousands of young black people on this weekend. It was just like the Freaknik in Atlanta, Georgia, used to.
Even record company moguls, artists, models, movie stars and
professional football and basketball players showed up.

"At this time we ask all passengers to turn off any and all electronic equipment . . ." the scripted message requested. This was
Tender and Goldie's first plane ride ever so they were attentive to
every safety instruction. They had seen and heard about too
many airplane crashes on TV to ignore their flight attendants.
Kat, a veteran of countless flights, simply ignored it all. It was
routine to her.

As the airplane began to taxi down the runway, preparing for
liftoff, it moved at such a speed, it pinned some passengers to the

back of their seats. The jet engines roared to life and lifted the giant aircraft off the ground.

Alone in her thoughts, Tender stared out her window. As the plane began to ascend, it reminded her of a roller-coaster ride. Only there were no sharp turns or sudden dips. The plane gently began to level off and the message was that it would be safe to unfasten their seat belts and move about the cabin. Continuing to look out her small port window, Tender marveled in amazement at Philadelphia down below. It was a tough town but from this bird's eye view, it looked so inviting and tranquil. This was a side of Philly she never thought she would see.

Midflight, Goldie had an anxiety attack. She began to hyperventilate and shake. A shot of Jack Daniel's calmed her and she fell asleep. Tender could have sworn she saw Kat slip Goldie some sort of pill in addition to the liquor. Goldie calmed down and it was nothing but smooth sailing afterward.

Some odd hours later, the coastline of Miami could be seen. From these friendly skies, Tender could see the natural beauty of the landscape: crystal clear, emerald green waters and sparkling sandy white beaches. It was truly breathtaking. She wished the whole hood could see what she saw. And appreciate God's green earth like she was.

Tender's mind drifted back to last night's deadly events and why Goldie was such a nervous wreck now. She hoped this excursion away from the streets of Philadelphia and all the drama would settle her down. Right now, she wasn't herself.

"We're now arriving in Miami. The weather is a seasonable eighty degrees and sunny . . ." the head stewardess announced. ". . . Enjoy your stay in Miami. And thank you for flying Air Tran . . ."

Sitting in business class, the girls were able to quickly exit the plane, long before the droves of passengers flooded the aisles, fighting each other for room to depart. After retrieving their luggage, Kat, Goldie and Tender walked through Miami International Airport like they owned it. It must have been a Philly thing, the way they carried themselves. Their struts suggested that they were somebody.

Strolling past the kaleidoscope of people, they were privy to many different languages, accents and dialects. Miami was an international melting pot, full of so many different ethnic origins.

Finally they made their way to the Avis rental car counter. Kat gave the counter person her driver's license and credit card. She was then handed a car rental agreement and the keys to a shiny black Jaguar. The other girls were not the least bit surprised— they knew Kat's style. She was going to live it up, at home and on the road, whether she was on the run or not.

They drove on the expressway, passing scenic downtown Miami. The city's skyline rivaled that of any city in the United States. In no time they reached South Beach and their hotel. Tall palm trees, exotic cars and scantily clad people greeted them, like a welcoming committee. Everywhere they looked they could see the bold and the beautiful. The Loews hotel was one of the most elegant, desirable and high-priced hotels on South Beach. It sat on a man-made hill with its powdery white finish. It slightly resembled a castle from a distance.

Kat wheeled her rental car up the hotel's oval brick driveway, coming to a stop at the entrance. She was met by a valet who helped remove their luggage while someone parked the car. Then the girls were escorted inside to check in.

"You have three rooms registered in your name, miss. My records show that one is a suite, and two adjoining rooms."

Kat merely nodded her head in agreement. After the receptionist magnetized the card keys, they followed the bellman to their rooms.

After settling in, Goldie and Tender paid Kat a visit. She had a large living room furnished in antiques, a massive mahogany bed and a fully equipped kitchenette. Each room was styled slightly different from the next. If this plush room didn't blow you away, then the breathtaking view of the beach and the Atlantic Ocean would.

Tender and Goldie were in awe. Tender couldn't wrap her head around how they had gone from last night and the confrontation with Jules to now. Not to mention how Kat could afford to stay here. But she'd soon find out.

From the balcony, they stood in amazement watching the wave runners, jet skis and windsurfers navigate the ocean's choppy waters. A little bit farther out they saw yachts gliding on the waters. It all looked like money, the likes of which they'd never seen before.

"Okay, I hada nuff of watchin' da fuckin' water," Kat said sarcastically. "It's time fa some action . . . Let's go shoppin' or sumthin'. I needa bathin' suit."

"So, we rollin' or what?" Tender said, to nobody in particular. "I'm wit whateva."

Goldie's response was slower. She couldn't think so easily about hanging out and having fun. She was still rattled and still coming off of her high, and the trauma of the night before.

"Y'all go 'head," Goldie urged them. "I'ma lay my ass down."

"Goldie, don't play yaself!" Kat called out. "C'mon now, ain't no time ta be tired. You ain't neva even been ta Miami and all you wanna do iz sleep? Dis iz da spot ta see and be seen. Man, you fuckin' up our whole day. You coulda stayed ya ass right in Philly, fa all dat . . ."

Goldie couldn't believe that Kat could be so business as usual. "Goldie, she's right. You should be too hyped ta sleep," Tender said. "It's on and poppin' down here. We might as well take in da sights and da sounds of Miami. You don't know when you'll be back? Or if you'll even be back? Goldie, c'mon now."

Tender was actually trying to hype herself as much as she was Goldie. She was trying to be in the present and not worry about things she could do nothing about.

"Aiight, Aiight!! I'm fuckin' comin'," Goldie said, caving in to their peer pressure. "You bitches talked me into it."

"Dat's whut'z up!" Tender cheered.

THEY HIT THE ARMANI EXCHANGE, Burberry, Prada, Versace and Todd Oldham stores. They would go back to Philly with some gear that nobody else had. They would turn heads and make jaws drop when they got home.

For now, they would head onto South Beach rocking the skimpiest suits they could find. Par for the course here where rarely would anyone be arrested for indecent exposure.

After getting their bikini lines and legs waxed back at the hotel, Kat, Goldie and Tender hit the strip. Kat wore a fire-red string bikini, a see-through sarong, matching Prada sandals, and a pair of lightly tinted Cartier frames, while Goldie wore a green one-piece, dark oval Christian Dior shades, a gold ankle bracelet, and high-heeled sneakers. Tender wore a two-piece Burberry swimsuit, matching tote bag and high-heeled flip-flops. A showcase that said, "What you see is what you can get, if the price is right."

They left the rental car in the garage at the hotel and walked. They got no more than a block away from their hotel before they were stopped by a couple of guys.

"Excuse me, miss," referring to Kat. "Would you mind posing for a picture with me?"

"Aiight, c'mon," Kat said. "But I betta not see dis shit on da Internet!"

"Naw, naw! baby girl. It ain't like dat," he quickly responded in a midwest accent. "Dis here fa me and da boys on lockdown."

As they snuggled close together, making themselves appear more like lovers than strangers, his friend snapped the picture with a disposable camera.

"Chuck, take another one just in case that don't come out," he instructed his friend. They had been up and down Washington Avenue and Ocean Drive snapping pictures of beautiful girls. Back home they would score major cool points with his boys.

When that was done, he made one more request. "Would y'all all take a picture wit me? Fa old times' sake?" he playfully asked, talking to Tender and Goldie like he had known them for a long time.

They willingly obliged him. He hugged Kat and Tender by their necks, since they were taller. Goldie stood in front of him since she was the shortest. His friend snapped two pictures and it was a wrap. The two parties went their separate ways.

The photo op request developed into a pattern that they quickly grew tired of. "Enough of this camcorders and camera shit," Kat finally said. So together they headed to the nearest rental shop and rented three motorized Honda scooters. Up and down the strip they rode. In and out of traffic they weaved, enjoying themselves. None of them had had this much fun in a long time. Tender and Goldie had never. They never had a chance to just play, even as children.

Night fell over Miami, leaving a beautiful fireball orange streak in the sky. When the sun went down, the freaks came out in droves. Black females and males combed South Beach looking for the best clubs and parties. During the day and well into the night, people passed out flyers promoting this or that party being thrown by some celebrity entertainer. Half the time, the other invited celebrity guests never showed up. It was just a gimmick to pack the club. You had to know somebody to get into some of the most exclusive parties or clubs. And even then, things didn't really get jumping till eleven P.M. and lasted well into the next morning.

Kat, Goldie and Tender found themselves on the outside looking in. Most clubs had long lines or VIP lists that you had to be on. Some were known to even reject celebrities.

"What y'all wanna do?" Tender asked nobody in particular. "Y'all wanna hit dis Missy Elliot party at Billboard? Ruff Ryder havin' an album release party fa Eve. Baby and Manny Fresh havin' a platinum party at Club Cristal." She read from the flyers she had collected.

"Well," Kat started, "dat Eve party iz out. Ain't no industry cats gonna be there. Not if we heard about it. They don't put dat type stuff out there like that . . ."

"Look, let's do sumthin'," Goldie insisted. "I'm tired. These high heels are killin' me."

". . . Not now, Goldie," Kat exclaimed. "Don't start no shit. We all got on heels jus' like you. You don't hear us complainin' . . . Listen, dis what we gonna do . . ."

Not willing to settle for the average party, Kat quickly devised a plan to get into one of South Beach's most exclusive clubs.

"C'mon, let's go!" Kat ordered.

After waiting for a few minutes on the back of a long line, Kat saw the precise opportunity she was looking for. Bolting smoothly to the front of the line, the girls blended in with a group of guys who looked like industry types. The bouncers were busy at the front of the line checking names on the VIP list and keeping order. By the time they reached the front of the line, the two parties looked like one. The girls took it a step further, keeping their pretend dates close, as if they were couples.

"Y'all, all tagether?" the big burly bouncer asked as he looked for their names on the VIP list.

"Yeah!" one lame guy replied. He was happy as hell to have a dime piece under his arm.

When the bouncer finally spotted their names on the VIP list, another bouncer opened up the velvet rope and together they all waltzed in. Needless to say, the other females on line were mad. They began hating on them, trying to tell the bouncers what they just did.

After determining that the guys they came in with weren't high rollers or producers, just studio technicians and recording engineers after all, the girls quickly brushed them aside, promising to get with them later.

The club was huge and packed. There were over a half-dozen bars. The dance floor was filled to capacity with partygoers getting their groove on. All Kat wanted to know was, where were the dudes with the money? She scoured the bars and tables for signs of overpriced bottles of champagne and platinum jewelry.

Spotting some potential players, Kat said, "You see those dudes right there?" pointing to a table where champagne flowed freely. "We need ta be fuckin' wit them! Fa real!"

The girls turned their attention to a table a few feet away where three heavily jeweled men sat. There was a flock of beautiful women already hovering around them. Money didn't seem to be a thing to them the way they popped bottle after bottle of Dom Perignon and Cristal. They possessed all the earmarks of hustlers.

"See the chicks sweatin' them? How we gonna get 'round them? What you wanna do, brody them?" Tender questioned. "We fuck 'round and be fightin' up in here."

"Yeah, how we gonna pull dat off?" Goldie chimed in.

"Follow me," Kat announced with confidence. "Watch this!"

As Kat stormed toward the table like a scorned lover, she secretly hoped that this stunt wouldn't backfire. Kat bumped, pushed and shoved her way through the crowd. She wore this wild look on her face that suggested she was crazy. Almost magically her path cleared.

"Damon!" she called out, saying the first name she could think of. "What da fuck you think you doin' wit all these bitches 'round you like that? . . . Naw, naw, nigga, I ain't goin' fa it. I'm about ta fuck one of these hos up!"

The deeper she went into her act, the faster the other girls began to disperse. This looked like some baby mama drama and they wanted no part of it.

The dudes looked at one another like who in the hell was she talking to. They were clearly amused by the way Kat was coming toward them and the other pretty girls were fleeing from them.

"Shawty, you know one a us?" one man asked.

"Naw!" Kat admitted, coming out of her act. "But I'm tryin' ta holla. And these bitches are in da way. You have ta excuse me, but I go hard fa what I want . . ."

"I see!" the man replied. "It's all good, girl. Even though you ran all my friends away here . . ."

"Fuck them chicken heads. Me and my peoples iz all the women y'all gonna need tanite . . ."

Goldie and Tender stood back and watched Kat work it.

"Where y'all from?" someone else asked, figuring they were from somewhere up north.

"Philly!" came the response.

"Um, uh! I knew y'all wasn't from here. Y'all straight gangster," he said, clearly impressed. "Shawty, since y'all went through all that trouble ta holla. Pull up some chairs and I'll show y'all a li'l southern hospitality. . . ."

Accepting their invitation, the girls gathered up three empty chairs and paired off. Making small talk, the group got to know one another better while the champagne flowed. Tender carefully nursed her drinks. Kat had schooled them earlier: They couldn't get pissy drunk and work these dudes. Tender gave her nothing to worry about. But Goldie wasn't sticking to the game plan. She downed glass after glass of champagne. As a consequence, Kat fumed.

Time was moving on and Kat was growing impatient. So she made her move. She got right to the point. She leaned over and spoke to her guy in a hushed tone. "Listen, what you and ya peoples tryin' ta get into?" she asked. "Cause it's gettin' a li'l late and me and my girlz iz tryin' ta do da damn thing, ya heard. We tryin' ta fuck. Straight up."

The guy rubbed his chin and smiled. Damn, this broad is bold, he thought. "Since you put it like dat. We can go back ta my hotel . . ."

". . . Be easy, playboy. Hear me out. Ain't nuttin' in dis world free. Na' mean? There's a small fee involved."

"Shawty, money ain't a thang," he replied. He had definitely seen her kind before. "Name ya price. Gimme a ballpark figure."

"A gee apiece," Kat said coolly, hoping she didn't overprice herself out the game. "And you got us all night. We'll be definitely worth ya while . . . Dat's chump change ta a player like you."

"Excuse me, fa a minute, Shawty. Lemme holla at my partnas . . ." he explained, then turned and whispered something in his friend's ear, obviously hipping them to the game. "Alright, let's get dis party started." He began to dig in his pocket and removed a large wad of cash.

"Yo, be discreet. Keep dat on da down-low," Kat urged him. She didn't want Goldie and Tender to witness this transaction. The man didn't give it a second thought, complying with her request. Kat smoothly cuffed the money and tucked it in her pocketbook. It was a done deal. The group left the club. Outside, a chauffeured white stretch Lincoln Navigator SUV awaited. As the limousine rode through the streets of Miami, headed for the guy's four-star hotel, the couples huddled among one another, flirting.

Behind closed doors, the guys turned out to be nothing more

than minute men. They were so intoxicated that they couldn't sexually function. One couldn't get hard, even after some serious fellatio by Kat. And the other two passed out as soon as they hit the bed. Goldie and Tender soon dozed off too.

Kat's devious mind was at work though. She couldn't sleep at a time like this, not with a golden opportunity staring her right in the face. As soon as she was secure with the fact that they were all fast asleep, she went through all their pants pockets. She relieved them of the rest of their cash and was tempted to take their jewelry too. But on second thought, she decided against it. They might come looking for her later. Then she'd have to leave town faster than she planned. And she wasn't ready to head back to Philly just yet. Tender, a light sleeper anyway, had only pretended to be asleep. So she saw Kat stashing on them.

Before the guys could awaken, Kat shook Goldie and Tender, and they eased out of the suite. They got a cab and went back to their hotel. Kat couldn't wait to count up the loot.

Back at their hotel, Kat pulled out the wad of bills. Tender was waiting to see if she'd do right by them. She broke off a few hundred dollars each for her and Goldie—chump change. Tender accepted her share and said nothing. She felt a stab in her gut.

# 10

THE NEXT DAY, the sun had reached its zenith, and the girls still weren't up. Their internal clocks were set to rise in the evening and nighttime. The air conditioner hummed steadily, sending mass doses of man-made Arctic chill throughout the hotel room. Tender lay curled up in the bed, underneath the covers. She never slept so well in her life.

The first thing that came to her mind when she woke up, though, was the stunt Kat had pulled. What happened to that three-musketeers ideology that Kat ran down, "All for one and one for all"? What happened to the idea of being free from pimps?

Tap! Tap! Tap! There was a light knock at her door.

Tender looked through the peephole. She hoped it was Goldie because she could use her company right about now. As she moved toward the door, she could feel the cold air on her nipples as they poked through her nightgown.

Tap! Tap! Tap! The knocks came again, this time a little louder. She had a sinking feeling in her stomach. "Relax! Hold ya horses! I'm comin'," Tender shouted. There stood a heavyset young black man on the other side of her doorway.

"Yo, it's Jay-dub," the guy quickly said. "Tender, right? Ya peoples, Kat, sent me up here. She said you'd know what it is . . ."

Kat had gotten up early and gone down to the hotel's lobby, pool area and bar, to solicit business.

"What? Shit!" she whispered to herself. "I'll be damned." Kat had some nerve, she didn't even holler at her to let her know what the deal was. At least she could have called her to let her know she was sending someone up to her room. Here she was, fresh out of bed, and face-to-face with a stranger. Could be the police for all Tender knew. She didn't want to open the door. But she did. She was here to make money.

"Aiight, I comin'," Tender said, stepping aside to let him by. She managed to muster up a fake smile. The guy looked around curiously, to make sure this wasn't a setup or some police sting. Secure in the fact that it wasn't, he relaxed, taking a seat on the edge of the bed.

"Big man, what you tryin' ta do? Pussy, brains, what?" Tender asked. This was going to be easy money. He was fat and, from past experience, she knew he probably had a small dick. In fact, judging by the looks of him, he hadn't seen his dick in years. "First thing first, big guy. I need my paper up front. Dependin' on what you want and how long it takes."

"Yo, Ma." The guy interrupted Tender. "I paid ya home girl . . . what's her name? . . . Kat! Yeah, I hit her off already."

"What?" Tender exclaimed, not believing him. She went to her purse and dug out her cell phone. Then she quickly dialed Kat's number. "Hello . . . Kat. Umm, dis cat dat you sent up here, said dat he gave you my paper already."

"Yeah, it's cool," Kat explained. "Now, handle ya handle. Fuck 'im or suck 'im . . . Just get rid of dat fat motherfucka. Hurry up, it's alotta niggas down here and they tryin' ta go."

Tender was still puzzled. "Why you holdin' my money? You ain't been doin' dat?"

"Look, Tender," Kat exploded, "stop fuckin' trippin'! That ain't 'bout nuttin'. I'm only holdin' ya money fa you, cause we don't know how these niggas rock . . . You ain't neva been nowhere. Soma these outta town niggas get down like dat. They might fuck you, then take their money back. So if I got it down here, then they can't do that. Aiight! Damn, don't get petty on me. I'm just tryin' ta look out and hold you bitches down. Da game don't stop cause we down here . . ."

"My bad! Thanks," Tender said and hung up her cell phone. Maybe she jumped the gun, she thought. She turned her attention back to the guy sitting on her bed. "It's all good . . . So, big man, what will it be?"

"Brains," he said.

Tender grabbed her purse to pull out KY jelly, spermicidal, and an assortment of condoms. She picked a regular nonlubricated condom.

"Aiight, big man, let's do dis. You on da clock," she announced, as she kneeled down in between his legs and unfastened his pants. A quick thought flashed through her head—she hoped he wasn't stinky.

Tender tore into the condom wrapper with her teeth and in one quick motion, she placed it in her mouth, while her other hand dug inside his pants to remove his penis. Just like she thought, he was working with nothing. As she went down on him, taking a quick whiff, she was grateful that he didn't have a strong body odor. There was nothing worse than sucking a stinking dirty dick. That made her nauseated.

Tender gave him a quick hand job as she worked the condom on. She yanked firmly but gently on his member. She tried to get him hard, to get his tiny penis to some size. He looked on, feeling somewhat ashamed.

Realizing this was as good as it was going to get, she took him in her mouth. She worked her tongue up and down his penis, swirling him around in her mouth. She licked him like she actually liked the taste of the condom.

At this point, the guy really began to get into it. He placed his hand on the back of her head and held it there, as she bobbed up and down. "Yeah, suck dat dick, bitch! Do it fa Daddy!"

Tender mused to herself, What dick? She picked up the pace, in an attempt to make him cum quicker. Even fully erect, he was small enough for her to deep throat him. Tender looked up and saw a facial expression of pure ecstasy. The contour of his face changed with every stroke. He was definitely on the verge of climaxing.

"Ssssss . . . Do dat shit . . . Ahhhhhhhhh!!!" he moaned, as the head of his penis swelled and he exploded semen into the condom. Forcefully, he pushed Tender's head into his crotch. This might have caused her to gag, had he been bigger. Instead, she stayed in that position till he released her.

"Aiight, big man, it's a wrap!" Tender said, as she climbed to her feet. "Let's roll."

Breathing heavily, he slowly began to get himself together. With his forefinger and thumb, he began to peel off the used condom. "Hey, don't drop dat on my floor," Tender warned him, as if she could read his mind. "Either drop it in da toilet or take it wit you." He shot her an evil smirk, walking toward the bathroom, carrying the condom by his two fingers, as if it were contaminated. The sound of a toilet flushing let Tender know exactly what he had done. After that he was gone.

Tender barely had time to freshen up before another man began knocking on her door. She did him. Then another. She went right along with the program, catering to each man's sexual needs. Next door, Goldie was equally as busy.

A customer they serviced invited Kat, Goldie and Tender to

an exclusive record industry party and they got all dolled up. Their aim was to catch a big fish tonight.

While Kat showered, Tender joined Goldie in her room, using the adjoining door. Tender noticed that she was unusually chipper. She had been so down in the dumps that Tender found this to be strange.

"My, aren't we happy-go-lucky today?" Tender joked. "Where dis come from, all of a sudden?"

"Ain't no particular reason. Maybe I woke up on the right side of the bed. Or maybe dis li'l change of scenery beats all dat drama back in Philly," she explained. "Life too short ta stay depressed all da time."

"Aiight, dat's what I wanna hear," Tender agreed. "But ummm . . . what's up wit dat stunt Kat pulled earlier? . . . Did she at least let you know what the deal was? I mean, I didn't know shit till some fat muthafucka come knockin' on my door . . ."

"Girl, we both in da same boat. I didn't know a damn thang till some nigga knocked on my door . . . But you know how Kat iz, always on da grind, chasin' dat paper . . ."

"While we wuz up here gettin' down fa our crowns, what was she doin'? Huh?" Tender questioned. ". . . Think about it. And by da way, did ya get ya money from her? I ain't get mine yet. And she ain't said nuttin' about it . . ."

All this talk about Kat, sex and money was beginning to ruin Goldie's high. She just wanted to forget about all this mess. Any way she could she tried to escape the reality that had become her life. She just wanted to feel happy for a change.

"Naw, she ain't gimme nuttin'. And ta tell you the truth, I ain't lookin' fa nuttin' either."

"What ya mean by that?" Tender questioned her. "Fuck dat shit." She gonna gimme minez. I ain't fuck all day fa free . . . What you sayin', Goldie?"

The rattle of the doorknob brought this conversation to an

abrupt halt. Kat was about to enter the room. Tender shot Goldie a look that said, "We'll finish this later."

"Glad you could join us," Goldie playfully remarked, as she opened the door. "Yo, Kat, I was just tellin' Tender 'em country boys sure do know how ta ball. Dat stretch Navi wuz no joke."

Down here in Miami everybody's a balla till they get back to they li'l hick towns. You can rent anything and everything down here. So niggas be stuntin'."

"But I don't think them niggas wuz fakin' any moves. They looked like they was gettin' it," Tender confessed, adding her two cents.

"Sometimes looks can be deceivin'," Kat said. "Ain't you ever heard dat old sayin'? Anyway, fuck 'em. They history. Gimme three new and a betta crew . . . Damn, you bitches sure iz takin' long gettin' dressed. Ya'll two iz like two old ladies. Always rappin'."

Tender smiled and said, "Yeah, let me go take my shower. Fuckin' wit Goldie, I got thrown off my square."

"Imagine dat," Goldie shot back. "Look where you at, in my room. You came over here ta talk ta me. Don't get it twisted."

"I don't care who said what when," Kat interrupted. "Can both y'all do me a favor and put a pep in ya step?"

"You got dat. Lemme go take my shower," Tender said. "Later on, I wanna holla at you, Kat. Aiight."

"'Bout whut?" Kat responded.

"Nuttin' important. I just wanna holla," Tender said, as she walked through the door that divided their rooms. "Matter fact, we can discuss dis now in my room."

"Aiight, no problem!" she stated, following Tender, who closed the door behind them. Kat took note that Tender wanted a private conversation.

"Well?" she announced. "What's up?"

"What's up wit my money?" Tender asked bluntly.

Kat couldn't believe the nerve of Tender. Who was she, to question her? She made her. Now wasn't the time or place for her to go off on Tender, though. They were still in trouble back home. At another time, she promised herself, she'd straighten her out.

"Oh, yeah. Dat kinda slipped my mind after I heard 'bout da party," she began. "But like I told you, I got you. I'm jus' holdin' on to it for now, cause I gotta safe in my room and y'all don't . . . Do you know these housekeepers be stealin'?"

Tender bought the lie. She ate it right up. Just as quick as her suspicions rose, they died. She overlooked the whole incident, choosing to give Kat the benefit of the doubt. Something deep inside her made her want to believe that they were real friends despite the way she could flip on her. Tender would leave it alone until they got back to Philly.

"Sorry fa comin' at you like dat," she apologized. "I'm trippin'. Fa a minute I thought you wuz tryin' ta play me."

"Naw, neva dat," Kat insisted. "We fam."

"Kool," Tender said. "I'm sayin' I jus' wanted ta know what da deal wuz. Dat's all."

"I feel you," Kat replied, lying through her teeth. "If I wuz you I probably wanna know da same thing . . ."

DRESSED TO KILL, Kat, Goldie and Tender hit the town. They were headed for Prestige Records' launch party. It was being held at a rented beachfront condominium. Only a chosen few would be allowed in. Somehow, Kat managed to come up with VIP passes for the event. It was on tonight. They were going to get a chance to rub shoulders with the rich and famous.

When they pulled up to the condo, they were greeted by a valet. He handed them a numbered ticket stub, then parked their car. From the looks of the parking lot, there were some moneymakers present. Bentleys, Porsches, BMWs, Lexuses and Mer-cedes-Benzes filled almost every parking space. The girls could barely contain themselves.

At the condo's entrance there stood two security personnel, of both genders. The girls had to submit to a light search, which was performed by the female security person. Everybody got patted down the same. It was usually a female who brought the weapons into the club undetected, for a male. Club owners and party pro-moters had smartened up and tightened their security. Even at events like this.

"Enjoy yaselves, ladies," the female security member said after Kat presented her with the VIP passes.

"Thank you. We will," Kat happily replied.

Even before they set foot inside the condo, the girls could hear music. It wasn't deafening but it was loud. The tunes were unfamiliar to the girls because these were new artists that were signed to the company's label. The sounds were hot, though.

Stepping inside the condo, the girls were greeted by a semi-packed house. Guys were standing in the long hallway, trying to put their mack game down. They maneuvered through the hall-way, drawing flirtatious stares, and occasionally brushing up against a few partygoers. Normally that would have been a prob-lem. In here it wasn't. Almost everybody in the party had some things going for themselves, and didn't want to jeopardize it over something so small as a bump against somebody they didn't know.

"Where ya headed?" Tender whispered to Kat.

"I'm tryin' ta find a place ta chill. Or the bar ta get a drink," she replied, leading the way.

"There goes da bar," Goldie announced.

They turned left and entered a barely furnished room. A small crowd congregated around the bar, waiting their turn to be served. The girls got in line.

"What will you have?" The white tuxedo-wearing bartender asked as they stepped up.

"Lemme get one virgin piña colada, a Long Island ice tea and an apple martini," Kat rattled off, ordering for everybody.

"Coming right up."

While they waited, the girls spun around to survey the party. They noticed lots of people dancing on the floor. This was the sign of a good DJ, one who can keep a party jumping. Continuing to look around, Tender soon elbowed Kat and Goldie. She had made a celebrity sighting. Ja Rule and Beanie Sigel were trading information on their two-way pagers. They were surrounded by their respective entourages. They casually glanced in their direction. Being from Philly, they were quite used to seeing stars. Just as well, since they didn't have a prayer of getting close to them, anyway.

"Here you are, ladies." The bartender handed them their drinks. "Enjoy."

"Thank you," they said in unison. The bar was open, courtesy of the record company. Kat noticed a tip cup, so she put a five-dollar bill inside. She was never one to knock somebody else's hustle.

Sipping on their drinks, the girls began to mingle. They blended right in as if they belonged there.

"Damn, this drink iz da bomb! Ole boy sure know what he's doin'," Goldie remarked. "Here, taste it, Kat."

"I'm good," Kat assured her. "Minez iz strong too . . . Listen, Goldie, don't go gettin' drunk. 'Member how toe up you wuz last time. You can't hold ya liquor."

Goldie thought, Fuck you! I'm grown. You ain't my mother! Yet she didn't dare utter these words aloud. She simply faked a smile, as if to say, "Alright, I won't."

"Yeah, Goldie, you wuz pissy last night," Tender added, not to insult her but to keep her on point. "Don't go there tanite."

"I'm glad you don't drink, Tender," Kat stated.

"It don't do nuttin' fa me. I don't need dat ta enjoy myself," Tender said. "It's jus' another bad habit."

Someone must have said something to the DJ, because suddenly he changed the music.

". . . I'ma hustler, baby, jus' want ya ta know . . ." rapper Jay-Z's mega hit began.

"Hoooo! Hoooo!" the crowd shouted, echoing their approval. A wave of excitement swept through the party and Tender and Goldie couldn't help but be caught up in it. Kat acted like she was too good to dance. So she stood there looking cute while Goldie and Tender put down their drinks and the two stepped right where they were.

If there was one thing Tender loved to do, it was dance. She quickly picked up a partner. He was good, too. They smiled and got on with it. Step for step they matched each other. Tender was having fun.

Suddenly, Tender had to pee. "Excuse me, I gotta go ta da bathroom. Can you tell me where it iz?" she said to her nameless dance partner.

"It's in da back!" he replied.

"Thanks." She broke across the room.

The line to use the bathroom was too long. She couldn't wait. She knew what to do. Every woman, and probably every man as well, knows that the men's room is never as crowded as the ladies'. So she stepped right over into the men's room. Just like she thought. Empty. Except for one man. But she didn't let that stop her.

"Yo, what da fuck is goin' on here?" he said, angling his head to get a look at her. You got the wrong room, mama."

"Calm down," Tender responded. "I ain't tryin' ta do you no harm. I jus gotta use da toilet real bad. Feel me?"

"Sis, you jus' can't bust all up in here like dat! Other people gotta take care they bizness too," the man said, as he shook the last of the urine out of his penis.

"Sorry. I couldn't wait. It was either run up in here or pee on myself," she explained, going about her business in a doorless stall.

Zipping himself up, the man decided to go for it and get a good look at girlfriend. Tender then got a good look at him too. His neatly cornrowed hair caught her eye first. She noted that they complemented his manhood rather than making him look feminine like some guys with braids. His blue baggy jeans, over-sized white T-shirt and spotless all-white Nike Air Force Ones gave him a thuggish appearance and a handsome one.

This man just happened to be Quinton "Q" Phelps, the CEO of Prestige Records.

Q was so low-key that his artists looked like they had more money than him. That suited him fine. He was too comfortable with his position to feel threatened by anything or anybody. He was also a stone-cold hustler who also happened to hail from North Philly. He had cleverly taken his illegal profits from the streets and founded an upstart record company. If he had one weakness, it was women. The more scandalous the female was, the better. Bad girlz were like forbidden fruit to him—the more he was told he shouldn't be with them, the more he desired them.

Bad girlz like his baby's mother. Their sex sessions were some kind of wonderful, but she was a drama queen, constantly creat-ing problems for him. If it wasn't one thing it was another. And he wasn't even dealing with her, relationship-wise, like that any-more. One moment of passion was causing him a lifetime of pain.

Tender had bad girl written all over her too—with her fine self, he thought. He felt himself getting aroused. "You ain't got no shame in ya game, huh?" he said to her.

She was already pulling herself together and heading for the basin to wash her hands. Another man came in and jumped back for a second when he saw her. "Pleeezzzze! You a big boy. I ain't got nuttin' you ain't seen before . . . Whateva ya name iz? I told you I had ta go bad. What you thought, I wuz playin' or sumthin'?" The man looked back and forth between Phelps and Tender. She went on. "I ain't got no problem wit you lookin', jus don't touch." The man almost forgot why he'd come into the rest room. Tender finished drying her hands like it wasn't nothing.

With a grin plastered across his face, Q followed Tender out of the door, admiring her shapely behind.

"Damn, sis, you caked up back there. Huh?" he said in a laughing manner. "Fa sheezie! . . ."

Tender was not the least bit amused.

"Yo, sis . . ."

"My name ain't sis," she responded.

"My name is Vanessa . . ." she joked. "Vanessa Del Rio."

"Dat's funny! You got dat one," he stated. "C'mon now, stop playin'. I'm serious."

Now the line of women she had jumped were checking Tender out, exiting the men's room with a man. "Aiight, my name iz Tender." Tender shot evil daggers with her eyes in response to the women's menacing stares.

"Hope you don't expect me to believe dat. What kinda name iz dat? . . . Tender . . . Though you do look a li'l young and innocent."

"Straight up! I'm fa real dis time."

Huh, if only you knew, Tender mused to herself. There wasn't a thing innocent about her anymore. "Dat's what they call me. And dat's what you'll call me till I say different."

"Oh, yeah? Anyway, you look familiar. Where you from?" he questioned.

"Whut'z dis? Twenty-one questions? You da po'lease or sumthin'?" she shot back.

"I don't know why you even went there wit dat. But I'm da

furthest thing away from a cop you'll eva see in ya life," he assured her. "Fa real!! You dissed me wit that comment . . . You just ruined my whole day . . ."

"Look, ummm," Tender stuttered. "Well, what's your name?"

"Q," he interjected.

"Yeah, Q. I apologize if I offended you. I wuz only playin'. It's not dat serious," she explained. "Anyway, I'm from Philly. And you?"

"Me, too! Damn, it's a small world . . . You don't know who I am? You neva heard of me? Q?" he answered, throwing his name out there again for good measure.

Tender took another look at his face. She thought long and hard. Then it came to her; she had heard of Q, a music mogul. *ca-ching*, the cash register in her head rang. In a chance meeting, she had come face-to-face with the man. She couldn't believe her luck.

"Wanna dance?" he whispered in her ear, while leading her to the middle of the makeshift dance floor. Only by holding hands did they manage to stay together. The crowd was mad thick.

Q was a very good dancer. His moves were fluent and his steps were on beat. She wondered, Was his sex as good as his dancing? having already made up her mind that she was going to give him some.

As they danced, Tender looked around the party trying to spot Kat and Goldie. Had she brought her cell phone with her, she would have gotten the numerous messages that they had left her. They had left the party with two dates. They'd see her back at the hotel. Tender wasn't a dummy though. She figured when she didn't see them that they were on a mission, chasing money. She was cool with that. It didn't bother her that she was there by herself. Because she was with a person she wanted to be with. She was in a position that either of them would love to be in.

Using every opportunity he got, Q ground his private parts

against Tender. She threw her body right back at him. There was no doubt to where all this sexually provocative dancing was headed.

"Let's get up outta here," he suggested, in a low seductive voice. "Go somewhere where we can be alone."

"Whateva," she replied simply.

They slipped out the party without drawing any attention to themselves. Q was glad that no one had seen him leave, especially another female who might have thrown a monkey wrench into his game.

Making their way to his car, Q hit his key ring alarm, deactivating it. His candy apple–red Porsche 911 two-seater glimmered under the moonlit sky. Sitting inside, Tender's nose was rushed with the smell of newness. Q had bought the ride in Philly and had it shipped down so he could style and profile.

As soon as he stuck his key in the ignition, the engine smoothly cranked up, and the instruments on the dashboard began to glow a fluorescent orange.

"Betta buckle up," he instructed her. "I drive fast."

"Jus' don't get us kilt. I'm too young ta die," she pleaded.

Q shifted the stick in reverse, backing up out of the parking spot. He shifted again and took off, leaving tread marks on the concrete. He drove past the valets, who stared at him like he was crazy. Tender's heart was racing as fast as the car. Q shifted from first to fifth gear, recklessly switching lanes from the city streets to the expressway. It was a miracle that they didn't get pulled over by the police.

He drove at crazy speeds, but handled the car well. He was a pro at driving from his earlier adolescent days as a car thief. There wasn't a cop in the city of Philadelphia who could keep up with him.

They arrived at a gated community in Coconut Grove. Relieved, Tender unglued herself from the seat and opened her eyes. She sighed, then looked over at Q, who smiled back at her.

"Told ya I drive fast. You thought I was playin'?" he remarked.

"Fast ain't da word. You's a nut behind da wheel. You drive like you gotta death wish or somethin'," Tender stated.

Q pulled into his reserved parking space, directly in front of a bungalow.

"We here," he announced, getting out of the car. "Let's go. Last stop!"

"Oh, you got jokes, huh?" Tender asked playfully, following him out of the car. As they walked, she noticed it had begun to drizzle.

He responded, "Only when I'm 'round cool peoples." He fumbled through his keys to open the door. This was some kinda different here, Tender thought. She wasn't treating this guy like a trick. She felt like she was on a date, for real. Was she trippin' or what?

"Dis you? You own dis?" she asked, as they entered the house. On second thought, she wished she could take that back. She didn't want to seem too nosy. She remembered that old saying, "If you gotta ask, then you can't afford it."

"Naw, I rented it. But fa da chunka change I paid for it, it should be mine," he admitted. "My label wuz in da process of puttin' da finishin' touches on some projects. So I thought it would be a good idea ta get my artists outta Philly. Dat way they could concentrate. Insteada hangin' out, runnin' da streets and losin' focus. Who you down here with?" he asked, looking at Tender.

"A couple of girlfriends."

"Where are they?"

"They doin' them and I'm doin' me."

Q stood for a minute, just staring at her. "Where ya man at? You too fine not to be on lockdown."

"Why you wanna know?" she asked as she toured the living room, checking out the place. "Probably with ya wifey."

He figured she was too streetwise to give him too much information. So he didn't press. He went into his kitchen. Outside, it began to rain, hard and fast. Tender looked out the sliding glass patio door from the living room to a scenic view of Biscayne Bay. She watched as the rain hit the waters. In the distance she thought she saw what appeared to be dolphins. It was magical. She felt like she was in a movie.

Something about this girl is different, Q thought. Or maybe not. Q was a sucker for a fine-ass woman. Aggressively. Anyway, he slid up behind her, cupping both her breasts with each hand, while gently kissing her on the neck. Goose pimples magically appeared on Tender's skin. He had found her spot. Her eyes began to close as she enjoyed this tongue bath. She began breathing heavily while she licked her lips. Seeing that he aroused her, Q continued to do what he was doing while undressing her. Assisting him, she turned around to face him, then she began passionately tongue kissing him as he tore at her clothes. Unable to contain herself, she clawed at his too.

Finally, they were naked, locked in each other's embrace. Clothes littered the floor around them. Never in her wildest dreams did Tender imagine that she'd yearn so lustfully for a man. It was as if she'd known him all her life. She had not even thought of mentioning money.

Tender and Q melted into the carpet, exploring each other's bodies with their hands. The rain shower had turned into a torrential downpour. The pounding of the raindrops against the patio floor intensified the mood.

"Q, let's do it out on da patio," she suggested. Tender always wanted to have sex in the rain. That was her yet-to-be-fulfilled fantasy.

"C'mon," he agreed, taking her by the hand.

Soon as they stepped through the sliding glass door, they were drenched by a sheet of rain. It didn't faze them. Q's manhood was so hard, it hurt. Throbbing nonstop, it stood at attention like a flagpole. Before they could even make their way toward a chair, Tender stopped Q in his tracks and dropped to her knees in front of him. She began to hungrily perform oral sex on him, no condom. Now he was well endowed. She had more than a mouthful; but there would be no deep throating him. She licked him in a loving way.

Soon they traded positions. But Q sat her on a lounge chair so he could put his head between her thighs and give her head. Q dived right into her neatly shaped triangle of pubic hair. With his fingers and tongue, he frantically searched her clitoris, parting the fat lips of her vagina. Finding her love button, he licked, nibbled and bit on it wildly. Her knees buckled and her body began to tremble—uncontrollably—and it wasn't from the chill of the rain. For the first time in her young life she had an orgasm. She cried out and held his head tightly against her body as the floodgates opened, releasing her sexual fluids. She couldn't believe what she was feeling.

Q stood up, walked Tender over to a table and bent her over. From behind he entered her, doggy-style. The rain and wetness from Tender's climax coated his penis, allowing him to slide right in. At first, she winced from the pain, till her vagina conformed to the shape and size of his manhood. Deeper and deeper he drove his penis inside of her. He enjoyed the view of her beautiful brown back and the sound of testicles slapping against her ass cheeks.

"AAAAhhhh," Tender exclaimed, as she climaxed for the second time.

He twisted Tender in every imaginable position, doing his thing to her. His stamina was incredible. Q guessed that Tender had probably been with young boys for the most part. He knew from experience that young boys didn't satisfy young girls. They were selfish in the bed, but not him. He always tried to make it a night for a woman to remember. He loved leaving them with something to talk about.

He pulled out and laid her down on an air mattress on the patio floor so he could enter her again from the front. By his rapid strokes, Tender could tell that he was about to climax now too. In the missionary position on the patio floor, he feverishly humped away.

"Don't cum in me," Tender pled, coming back to her senses. She knew damn well she was in no position to raise a baby. "Pull out and bust off on me. Put it on my titties. I wanna see it." She wanted to stop him but not shut him down.

He gave her no inclination as to whether he heard her or not. He was in a sexual trance, hypnotized by her vagina. He kept right on going till he felt a strong surge shoot from his testicles, through the length of his penis, swelling the tip of it. Then, he quickly withdrew from her. He gripped his manhood with one hand as he ejaculated a load of white semen all over Tender's upper body. Then he collapsed on top of her, completely drained, completely soaked.

# 11

KAT, TENDER AND GOLDIE were back in Philadelphia, making their way to baggage claim. Along with the rest of the passengers, they watched as suitcases, travel bags and duffel bags went by on a conveyer belt. After that, they hopped in a taxi. As the moments progressed, more and more they began to think about all the drama that led to them fleeing the city in the first place. This had been no ordinary vacation. Miami had been a nice fun diversion and a temporary escape, but now it was back to reality. Fun and games were over. No telling what they were stepping back into.

There's no place like home, though, Tender had thought as the plane landed at the airport. She had the city of Philly running through her veins. Miami was a nice place to visit, but she didn't want to stay. Philly was home, with its harsh winters and tough streets—it was all she knew. The glitz and glamour of South Beach wasn't real to her. It was just too make-believe. She'd take the gritty, grimy, fast-paced, crime-infested streets of Philly any day. That was life to her—pain, suffering and loss. She didn't grow up with a silver spoon in her mouth. She knew tough times didn't last; tough people did. She thought about Q and how they had promised each other that they would stay in touch. He had her cell number and called within days. She came clean, laying her cards faceup on the table, and told him she was a stripper. He seemed to take the news well. He didn't put her down. He even went so far as to say, "What you do don't make you who you are." She told him that she planned on using the game as a stepping-stone to better things. If she played her cards right, and hustled hard, she'd be able to open a hair salon. She planned on using the game and not letting it use her.

He took her to dinner a week later and ended the night by giving her a platinum chain and pendant, with a capital *P* encrusted with diamonds, which represented his record company's logo. He gave her this as a token of his friendship. Tender was shocked. After that, she found herself counting the minutes, hours and days until they saw each other again.

TENDER HAD MENTIONED to Goldie and Kat that she'd met a guy from Philly, but hadn't said too much about him. Kat started getting the picture when she saw the bling-bling. If she was getting gifts like that, he had to be paid.

"Damn, dat nigga really blessed you," Kat exclaimed, as she enviously stared at Tender's necklace. "Either he must really be ballin' or you really rocked dat nigga world."

"Maybe it's a li'l of both," Goldie commented. "You neva know. Maybe Tender got dat whip appeal. Huh?"

"Maybe," Tender joked. "I ain't sayin'. Ancient Chinese secret. Been in my family fa generations . . . Eat ya heart out!"

Whip appeal my ass! Kat thought. Da bitch iz lucky. Dat's all!

"I ain't mad atcha!" Goldie said.

"How much you think dat chain costs?" Kat asked.

"I don't know. I ain't ask. It was a gift. You're not suppose ta ask those kinda questions . . . As long as it's real, I could care less," Tender stated.

"Still," Kat countered, "if I were you, I'd have it appraised by a jeweler. Just ta know what kinda change you lookin' at if you should havta sell it."

But you're not her! you greedy, conniving bitch! Goldie mused, while hiding her thoughts behind a fake smile.

"I ain't into dat. How I'm gonna sell sumthin' somebody gave me?" Tender said.

"Fuck dat, you don't know dat nigga like dat. I'd sell it inna heartbeat . . ." Kat replied. "Let dat had been me . . . You need ta step ta ya bizness and play dat nigga how he suppose ta be played. You bitches runnin' 'round here bein' kindhearted and shit . . . If you can't handle him, pass 'im off and I'll show you how it's done."

Goldie could hear the larceny in Kat's heart already. There was no mistaking it. She was envious. That was typical of Kat; she wanted hers and yours too. She wanted everything for herself.

"Naw, dat's aiight!" Tender replied coolly. "I'm good. I got dis."

"Jus' jokin'," Kat lied. "Do you."

Tender shrugged it off, and continued to engage in conversation. Idly they chitchatted about their trip to South Beach, and what went down when they parted company. About who did what. What went down behind closed doors. Tender made a crucial mistake of mentioning Q's huge member and bragging on how good he was. Goldie just brushed her comments aside, thinking nothing of it. But Kat absorbed it, wanting to know more details. She was hanging on Tender's every word. She filed them away in her memory bank for later use.

Tender forgot the rule that said, "What goes on in Miami stays in Miami." She would later regret having said anything. Still, she didn't talk about how she was feeling Q, not as business, but as a person. No man had shown her as much respect as he had and it was still blowing her mind.

Shortly after settling in, Kat left the house to get her truck washed. Tender made herself comfortable, slipping into her pajamas, stretching out on the couch, watching reruns of *Jerry Springer*. This was the funniest talk show on TV. She never could understand why people would come on the show and air their dirty laundry in front of a national audience of millions. Maybe they wanted a free trip to Chicago or they were just plain stupid. Whatever the case may have been, Tender was glued to the tube, anxiously awaiting some new juicy rumor, embarrassing gossip or startling secret they had to reveal. One thing was for sure, the show never seemed to run out of foolish guests to make her laugh.

Meanwhile, in the bedroom, Goldie busied herself writing an entry in her diary. Tender peeped in on her and Goldie didn't even notice. Tender swore one day she'd read exactly what was so important that she had to document it every day. Goldie was her friend though, and she really couldn't violate her like that, not under any circumstances, never in a million years. Whatever she was writing was her business. She remembered the old saying, "Curiosity killed the cat." She didn't want them to fall out behind her being nosy.

As Tender entertained herself by watching that nonsense television, Goldie wrote. She also pulled her Bible out of her nightstand drawer. It had been given to her at a church soup kitchen some time ago, when she lived on the street. She fell into a solemn mood as she pored over the scriptures, verse after verse, chapter after chapter. Lately she was overcome by a strong urge to reconnect with her spiritual roots, to cleanse her soul.

"Proverbs thirty-one, verse thirty-one: Charm is deceitful and beauty is passing; but a woman who fears the Lord, she shall be praised . . ." Goldie rambled aloud as she quoted the verses.

"Huh?" Tender shouted back. "Goldie, you called me?"

Goldie ignored her. She was in a trancelike state. "Proverbs twenty-three, verses thirteen and fourteen: Do not withhold correction from a child. For if you beat him with a rod, he will not die. You shall beat him with a rod, and deliver his soul from hell . . . Proverbs twenty-two, verse six: Train up a child in the way he should go, and when he is old he will not depart from it."

These verses really hit her where it hurt. Her mother had a right to beat her the way she had, she thought. All she was trying to do was raise her right and she had rebelled. There it was right in front of her in black-and-white, in the Bible. God had decreed it.

After getting no response from Goldie, Tender waited for a while, continuing to watch the madness of *Jerry Springer.* A fight was about to break out and she didn't want to miss it. Then something told her to walk back to the bedroom.

"Goldie, what's up? You aiight? I thought I heard you say something," Tender said, as she entered the room.

"I was jus' readin' da Word," she answered. "I didn't realize I was dat loud . . . umm, Tender, can I ask you somethin'?"

"Yeah, what?" Tender replied.

"You believe in God?" she asked.

"Yeah," Tender quickly replied. "Why?"

"Why? . . ." she repeated. "Cause we livin' a life of sin. What we doin' is wrong. And I know it and you know it. Ain't no two ways about it . . . I can't take it no more. I want out."

Tender looked directly into Goldie's eyes, and what she saw scared her. If it was true that the eyes were the windows to the soul, then Goldie was living in a wrecked building. Her eyes were tired, sad, crazed. Like her spirit had been ripped up.

"Goldie, where all dis come from? What, you been speakin' to Kat's sista or somethin'? I neva heard you talk like dis before. What's gotten into you?"

"I'm gettin' tired a livin like dis!" Goldie stated. "Dis ain't livin'. Dis ain't life . . . Dis ain't da life fa me . . . or you . . . We need ta get outta here. Before somethin' else happens. I ain't tryin' ta die in dis state. I ain't tryin' ta die in a state of sin."

Goldie came across sincere, but more than a little bit para-noid. Tender thought, This bitch is trippin'. She done lost her fuckin' mind! Goldie hadn't deliberately chosen this life. It chose her. She hoped her friend wasn't going off the deep end.

"Goldie, Goldie, slow down. You sayin' a lot at one time," she expressed. "Now I don't know much 'bout da Bible, but from my understandin' we all sinners in one way or anotha. Whut's dat verse in da Bible, 'Ye who iz without sin, let him cast da first stone . . . ' Like Tupac said, 'I wuz given dis world I didn't make it . . . ' I'ma keep it real wit you, we all do what we gotta do. E'rybody doin' them fa they own individual reasons. Dat don't make it right, but . . . understand da circumstances, God gotta under-stand. If he's a lovin' God and a forgivin' God, he'll see what type of people we really are . . . I'm not a bad person, jus' 'cause I do bad things. You think I wanna dance fa strange men, butt-naked? You think I wanna have sex fa money? Dat took a lot ta get use to. I block it out, pretend it ain't me and I'm not there. I'm jus' doin' what I got to do fa now. I know it'll get greater later. . . ."

"My mother . . . God bless her soul," Goldie began, "taught me right from wrong. She taught to cover my private parts. And to wear loose-fitting clothes. She taught how to carry myself like a lady, the young lady dat I am. She taught how to respect myself . . . If she could see me now? She'd be ashamed at the whore I've become. She's probably rollin' over in her grave as we speak . . . I don't even know why I was born. Why was I put on dis earth? Ta curse my mother? I wish God jus' put me outta my misery. . . ."

"Goldie, stop talkin' like dat," Tender warned her. "You scarin' me. Now, it ain't dat bad. You been through a lot and I been through a lot. But we still here. We still alive and kickin'. We survivors. They can't break us. Don't let dis shit break ya spirit. Soon, we gone come up. We gone find a betta way. God does not place too heavy of a burden on nobody. Believe dat . . . We jus' gotta hold on and weather the storm. Make it through these rainy days. We wuz put here fa a reason. What? I don't know. . . ."

They both fell silent as the weight of Tender's words began to sink in. Tender leaned against the wall, lost in thought, while Goldie's shoulders slouched over. Her facial expression seemed to say it all: She looked defeated.

Depression had taken hold of Goldie. She was crying out for help but her call fell on deaf ears. She had to get out, get away from this life. Any other time Tender could cheer her up, snap her out of her funk. If it hadn't been for Tender's positive presence, she would have fallen to pieces a long time ago. This time though, her burdens, worries and fears were bigger than that. No pep talk could bring her back.

"I swear ta God," Goldie cried, "I hate dis shit! I wish I wasn't born . . . I wish my mother were still alive . . . I wish I was dead. . . ."

She burst into tears. Tender rushed to hold her in her arms. She felt her pain, but was powerless to stop it. Goldie's feeling came from within her soul. She was mortally wounded.

"Goldie, don't say dat no more. You hear me? You all I got . . . and I luv you. Don't forget dat. I gotcha back, even if nobody else do. Remember that. . . . Be strong, girl. Do it fa me, . . ." Tender pleaded.

". . . I wanna stop strippin'. Dis ain't me! Dis ain't fa me, . . ." Goldie stated.

"I know, Goldie. I know . . . I don't wanna do it no mo' either, Tender confessed. But . . ."

"But what?" Goldie asked. "Gimme one good reason."

"Goldie, I need money. I'm tryin' ta open a bizness someday soon. I can't jus' walk away. Not now . . . I'm almost there. . . ."

"Tender, do you know Kat would leave ya ass flat in a heart-beat? She's not ya friend. She's a great pretender. Fuck her, let's leave. Leave her ass here by her miserable self . . . There's no betta time than now. . . . If you don't go now, then you neva will. . . ."

"Dat's not true. I want out jus' as bad as you. But we gotta think dis thing out. We can't jus' leave like dat."

"You do hair real good, Tender. You could get a job in jus' about any beauty parlor in the city. And you know it too. You jus' don't wanna try."

"But I don't have a license yet. I'll get there though. Don't worry 'bout dat. We'll make it. Together. God'll take care of us, Goldie. It'll be hard fa sure."

Tender believed in God, but she didn't have a lot of faith in Goldie's holy plan. She knew that God helps those who help themselves. It took more than blind faith and some prayer to receive a blessing. For them to strike out on their own without any concrete plan was nothing short of stupid. Almost like a back-woods preacher who sticks his hand in a poisonous snake pit, then, when bitten, he refuses medical treatment, thinking his faith in God alone will save him. No, Tender couldn't work with that. Despite what Goldie thought, she wanted out of the strip-ping game. She was growing tired of the grind, irate customers, pimps, and the cliques of girls in the club. She didn't want to burn out like Goldie, but she caved in.

"Aiight, Goldie, I'll go," Tender agreed, surprising even her-self.

Goldie squeezed Tender tightly. She was relieved. She didn't want to go it alone.

"We gonna make it," Goldie assured her. "You'll see. Once we stop stripping, a whole new world will open up to us, watch. . . ."

Tender reluctantly went along with the program. But in the back of her mind, she wondered how they were going to break the news to Kat. She was surely going to flip out when she heard this.

As Kat steered her truck through the streets of Philly, she couldn't get Q off of her mind. Especially not after all the things Tender told her about him. It didn't matter that she didn't know him or hadn't even seen him. He was paid and that was all that mattered. She fantasized about what a man of his stature could do for her. If she got a crack at him, she promised herself that she would go all out. And for her efforts she was quite sure she'd be living large.

With her thoughts focused on Q, she inadvertently ran a stop sign. Kat didn't even realize it until she saw the red lights of a po- lice car flashing in her rearview mirror.

"What da fuck they want now?" she cursed aloud, banging on her steering wheel. She thought he was stopping her just to mess with her. "Damn," she cursed after she looked and realized she had run a stop sign. Fuck it, she thought, just write me a ticket and let me go about my business. I don't have any time for this.

Kat pulled over to the curb, switched her car off and placed her hands in full view. She knew the routine. She didn't want to become a statistic of some nervous cop. She knew how quick the police were to brutalize and kill black motorists in the hood.

The cop seemed to be taking his time approaching her vehi- cle. She glanced in her rearview mirror to see what he was doing. He appeared to be on his radio calling the stop in or running her license plates. Pretty soon, two more squad cars emerged on the scene. They seemed to swarm like bees to honey. This was more than a routine traffic stop.

The police ran Kat's license plates and saw that she was wanted for questioning in connection with an unsolved murder. Taking no chances, the cops boxed Kat in, closing every avenue of escape. Kat's heart began to pound as they approached with weapons drawn. Now she could only wish it was a simple traffic violation ticket.

"Miss, would you mind stepping out of the car? Slowly," the white cop cautioned.

"What's da problem, officer?" she asked in her nicest voice. "What's all dis for? I didn't do nuttin'?" Y'all act like I'm America's Most Wanted or somethin'."

"Miss, if you would be so kind as to slowly exit your vehicle. Step around to the front of the car, and place your hands on the hood," he repeated slowly. "I'll explain everything shortly."

Kat did as she was instructed to do. In slow motion she moved, careful not to make any sudden motions, knowing in the back of her mind she was a half second from making the daily news, it took everything in her power to control herself. She thought she'd never see the light of day again.

They roughly slapped the cuffs tightly on her small wrists, damn near cutting off any circulation of blood. A female cop came along, and quickly patted her down for weapons or contraband. Finding none, they began to search her car. That turned up nothing too.

"Why am I bein' arrested?" she shouted. "What did I do? You can't jus' handcuff me and take me away. I know my rights—"

"Miss, are you Katrina Carter?" the cop asked, knowing damn well she was, having seen her driver's license.

"Yes, dat's me . . ." she cried.

"You're wanted downtown for questioning for a homicide that happened a few weeks ago. We have reason to believe this vehicle was at the scene of the crime. If you did nothing, then you have nothing to worry about. The detectives just want to talk to you. After that you will be free to go," he announced.

She had to face the music, alone. The bad thing was, she wasn't even the shooter. And since she wasn't, she sure wasn't taking a murder rap for somebody else who was. It wasn't in her nature to be the fall guy. If she was going down, then everyone was coming with her.

The detectives downtown at the station house addressed Kat as if they were friends. They were feeling her out, probing her for information. They had nothing on her, but they were following up on a lead. She immediately assumed the worst.

"A confidential informant has placed your truck at the scene of the crime. Where were you at the time and date in question?" the detective asked.

"Listen," Kat explained. "I told you already dat I'm a stripper. I work late hours. My car iz usually always parked on dat block. It wuzn't me! I didn't kill nobody!"

"I didn't say you did," the detective stated firmly. "Said that you were in or around your car at the time of the murder. You saw something, you know something, that could possibly make you an accessory to murder. Do you understand what kind of time that charge carries? Don't you have a son? You can't raise him from jail."

He continued, "Katrina, or is it Kat? I don't know you, sweet-heart. Never seen you before a day in my life. We didn't just run you in 'cause we felt like it. The streets are talking. And they're calling you Killer Kat."

She was beginning to sweat bullets. "It wuzn't me!" she stated for the record. "I ain't do it. It wuz . . . It wuz Goldie! Goldie kilt 'im! Yeah, she shot 'im!"

This was easier than they thought. From the looks of Kat, they had assumed she was a tough cookie, that maybe she'd be a hostile witness.

"Who's Goldie?" the detective asked, as he leaned closer in an attempt to make sure he heard every word she said. "What's her real name? She a friend of yours? Where does she live?"

"She's some girl from da club . . ." Kat said, downplaying their relationship. "I give her a ride home every now and then. She's an associate of mine. I know her from workin' in da club. I think her real name iz Gloria . . . Gloria Cruz. Yeah, dat's it. I seen her ID before."

"You're lying!" he insisted. "Now, you better not be bullshittin' me. . . . So help me God, I'll have the judge throw the book at your ass. You understand me?"

Kat merely nodded her head in agreement. They had her shook. Right now, she would tell on God if she could.

"Now where does she live?" the detective demanded. "I wanna answer now!"

Kat didn't dare further incriminate herself by telling them the truth now, that she resided at her house. That was perjury, she thought. She knew she could go to jail for that. "I dropped her off in north Philly, on Fifteenth and Styles—on the corner, cause her boyfriend don't like nobody to know where they live."

"You're lying!" the detective insisted. "You made this whole story up. You think I'm stupid? Keep tryin' to protect somebody. And when we find them, I bet they'll roll over on you. You better be tellin' the truth, young lady. Or you're gonna be in a world of trouble. . . ."

"I'm not lyin'!" Kat cried. "Tellin' da truth. I told y'all everything. . . ."

Now it was the other detective's turn, his opportunity to play the good cop. It was classic police maneuver, divide and conquer theory. He pulled his partner to the side. He pretended to be whispering, but he made sure he talked loud enough for her to hear.

"Listen, Bob," he began, "take it easy on her. For Christ sakes, she's a woman. I think she's tellin' the truth. Now, why don't you go cool down. Go get yaself a cup of coffee or somethin' . . . Let me handle this. You're about ta have a freakin' heart attack, fa cryin' out loud."

"Alright, Josh," his partner said, pretending to regain his composure. "You take it from here. I'll be down the hall going over some files."

"You do that," he said, patting him on the back.

Then he turned his attention back toward Kat, who was nervously shifting in her chair.

"Is there anything I can get for you?" he asked politely. "Soda? Coffee? Tea? . . . How 'bout a bottled water?"

"No, thank you," Kat stated. "Only thing I want iz outta here."

"I hear you. Just hold ya horses. We'll only be a few more minutes," he assured her. "Now listen, the way this works is, you help me and I help you. *Comprender?*"

"Yeah," she replied.

"Now, would you be willin' to sign a sworn statement on everything you just told us?" he asked.

"If it'll get me outta here. Yeah!" she admitted.

"Okay," he said, pulling the form along with a pen out of a drawer. "Now, let's take it from the top. You said that a person by the name of Gloria Cruz, I believe, is responsible for the murder. Am I correct?" The detective pushed several other pieces of paper in front of Kat for her to sign and write her statement. He smiled. Now all there was left to do was find the perpetrator.

As he prepared to wrap up this interrogation, his partner reentered the room. "How's it goin'?" he asked.

"Everything is A-OK." His partner beamed. "Do me a favor, Bob. Would you run down to the courthouse and ask the judge to issue a warrant for the arrest of a Gloria Cruz?"

Kat sped home but time was not on her side. She knew she had to get rid of Goldie. She had to distance herself or else she was going down with her. If the police knew she lied to them and was harboring a fugitive, she would be in some serious trouble. Goldie had to go. Kat felt no remorse, no shame in what she had done. She reasoned, if the shoe were on the other foot, Goldie'd do it to her. She just beat her to the punch.

When Kat entered the house, the flush look on her face told Tender something was very wrong. She looked like she had seen a ghost. Tender had been wondering how she was going to break bad news to Kat. But Kat dropped the bomb on her first.

"Where's Goldie at?" Kat demanded to know as her eyes frantically searched around for her.

"She's in da room. Why? Whut's up?" Tender questioned.

"Whut's up?" Kat repeated. "I'll tell you what's up! Da fuckin' po-lease iz lookin' fa her ass. They know she shot Jules. Dat bitch iz hot!!!"

"Whut?" Tender said, dumbfounded. "How you know?"

"Cause, they fuckin' pulled me over and ran my ass in. I wuz sittin' in da precinct fa hours . . . They wuz askin' me lotsa questions 'bout her . . . They even know her real name."

"Whut?" Tender mouthed unbelievably. "How they know all dat?"

"How I'm 'pose ta know?" Kat shot back. "It's they damn job. They get paid ta know shit . . . They investigate . . . Now where's Goldie? Her ass has gotta go, right now! She's hotta than fish grease . . . Goldie!!!"

When Kat reached the back room, Goldie had just finished packing the last of her things. "Goldie! Don't you hear me callin' you?" Kat shouted. "Look, you gotta go. Da fuckin' cops are lookin' fa you. They know . . ."

"Know 'bout what?" she asked.

"They know 'bout Jules! . . . They know you shot 'im . . ." Kat had a wild look in her eye. "I don't need dis shit! Girl, you gots ta get da fuck outta here. Befo' they run up in here. I'm not goin' ta jail fa nobody . . ."

Suddenly, Goldie burst into tears. Her time was running out. She, who never intentionally set out to hurt anyone. Yet, all she seemed to attract was trouble. And all she seemed to create was problems for herself. To her, it seemed as if she incurred the wrath of God.

"I'ma turn myself in," she sobbed. "I'ma murderer. I belong in jail wit da rest of da savages. . . ."

"No, don't do dat," Tender pleaded. "Jus go on da run till we can scrape up enuff money ta pay for a good lawyer . . . Goldie, you ain't got no record. You can beat dis. We ya witnesses, we saw everything. We'll testify fa you . . ." It was self-defense.

"I may be innocent in da court of law, but I'm guilty in God's eyes. Remember the Ten Commandments? 'Thou shall not kill' . . . Dis ain't da first time—"

Tender didn't know what to make of this. "Hurry up! You gotta go," Kat frantically yelled. "Get ya things and go. Befo' it's too late . . . They might come raid my house. They'll take my son away from me and put 'im in a home. Oh, my God . . ."

Kat quickly scribbled a phone number on a small piece of paper, then reached into her pocketbook and removed a wad of cash. She shoved the couple of hundred dollars in Goldie's hand. Then she practically dragged her through the house toward the door, bags and all.

". . . Tender, don't jus stand there, call a cab," Kat instructed her.

"Where am I goin'?" she managed to ask. "I ain't got nowhere ta go."

"Ya goin' ta New York. It's a big city, they'll neva find ya there," Kat said. "Don't worry, I got some peoples up there. They'll look out fa you. When you get there all you gotta do iz call da number on dat piece a paper I gave you. . . ."

Kat had some people in New York alright, and they were just like her. They'd use Goldie for their own purposes. They would finish the job that Kat had started, that was destroying Goldie's life.

"Tender, come wit me . . ." Goldie pleaded. "Pleezzze!!! I can't make it by myself. . . ."

There was a long painful silence for what felt like an eternity. Goldie looked so sad and pathetic that it broke Tender's heart.

"She can't go wit you," Kat snapped, putting a quick end to that notion. "Then she'll be in jus' as much trouble as you. Then what good will she do you? Huh? She gotta stick around till things cool off. She'll join you later. And so will I."

"But. But," Goldie sulked. "Tender—"

The noise from the cab's horn interrupted their conversation. This was music to Kat's ears. It couldn't come quick enough for her. She rushed her out the door. As she led her, Goldie turned and looked at Tender as if it were her last time seeing her. A look of pure sadness was etched across her face. She was a lost soul.

Tender never felt so helpless. She wanted to help her but she didn't know how. She was caught up too, just not as bad as her friend. Her best bet was to stay put. She could help her more on this end by hustling up the money for a lawyer, than to join her on the run.

"Goldie," Tender said, feeling tears well up in her eyes, "I luv you—"

"You gotta go," Kat announced as she pushed her out the door. "Hurry up, befo' the cab leave you—"

With that, she gave Goldie a strong shove in her back, pushing her out the door. She practically slammed the door in her face. Kat didn't even have the decency to say good-bye.

# 12

B AA-LING! *Baa-ling! Baa-ling!* Tender's cell phone begged to be answered. She purposely ignored it. She didn't feel like talking to anybody, for business or pleasure. She was shut down. Ever since her girl Goldie left, things hadn't been the same. She felt like a jigsaw puzzle with a missing piece—incomplete. She had stepped back to examine herself since Goldie's sudden departure, contemplating her way of life. There had to be another way to eat, a better way.

She started to turn the phone off, but she was secretly hoping Goldie would call her. She hadn't heard a word from her since she left and that worried her. She finally answered the phone.

"Hello!" she snapped.

"What's poppin', stranger?" A man's voice spoke. "You sure iz hard ta hit on da hip! What, you tryin' ta tell me somethin'? It wasn't good?"

"Who dis?" Tender replied, unable to place the voice. She thought this was a date.

"Oh, you don't know me wit my clothes on? Huh?" the man

asked. "Well, here's a clue. Miami. Rain. Patio. Sex. Me, breakin' you off. You, lovin' e'ry minute of it . . . Need I say more?"

"Q." She exhaled into the phone, as if a burden had just been lifted. Immediately the bass left her voice. Her spirits raised up.

"Holla! Dat's right! Dis da boy Q. Girl, you recognize a playa when he's in ya presence," he said jokingly. "Fa a minute dere, you had me worried. I thought somebody else wuz gettin' my time. You know how these jokers do . . . I'm often imitated, but neva duplicated. Didn't know bein' me could be so complicated . . ."

Q was a welcome diversion but he had a hell of a sense of humor. Life was too short and, at times, too serious for her.

"Boy, you are a piece of work," Tender commented. "Why you ain't call me? You God's gift ta women? You ain't got it like dat! Q, I missed you . . ."

"Slo, slo, slo down!" He began chanting the verses from a popular rap song into the receiver. "Tender be easy. Everything is still everything . . . I've been really busy wrapping up these projects. Meeting wit marketing and promotional teams. You know my business comes first. Can't nobody run it like I will. But you know what they say, all work and no play . . . I told you I wuz gonna holla as soon as I got clear, and I'm a man of my word."

"I see. I'm sorry fa trippin' like dat. I'm goin' thru somethin' . . . It ain't got nuttin' ta do wit you," she explained. "I been trippin' since my peoples left . . . she wuz like a sista ta me. We wuz dogz—"

"Who's this? Damn, what she do, die?" he asked seriously, detecting a hint of sadness in her voice.

"Naw, nuttin' like dat," she replied. "It's a long story wit a whole lotta drama. . . ."

"I'm sorry ta hear dat, but what you doin' now? If you want, I'll shoot over there and pick you up. Take you out ta eat or sumthin'? Get ya mind right . . . How dat sound? Is on and pop-pin' or what?" he said.

"Fa sheezie. Get here wit da quickness, aiight?"

"Gimme like twenty minutes. I gotta handle sumthin' right quick. Then I'll come by and scoop you," he stated.

"Sounds like a plan ta me."

She went to the bathroom to freshen up. The whole time she prayed that he would indeed show up. She knew how quickly men can get sidetracked, especially guys that run the streets. She needed an escape from the house, Kat and the bad karma that was around. She mused to herself, boy, things are going from sugar to shit.

*Bonk! Bonk!* The car horn alerted Tender to Q's arrival. The knight in shining armor was here. Kat must have heard the noise at the same time. She came out of her room to investigate.

"Dat's fa you?" she questioned. "Who's dat? . . . Where you goin'?"

"Out!" Tender replied flatly.

"Who dat? Dat's Q?"

"Yeah, dat's him," she replied with an attitude. "Why?"

"Oh, nuttin' . . . I mean niggas ain't been pullin' up in fronta here lookin' fa you . . . I thought maybe . . . Maybe it wuz fa me. Dat's all." Kat lied, trying to hide her intentions.

"Naw, he hollerin' at me," Tender remarked smartly. "Don't wait up."

"Have fun. And don't do nuttin' I wouldn't do." Though her voice was cheerful, if Tender would have turned back around at that very moment, she would have seen the hate in Kat's face. What Kat would trade to be in Tender's shoes right now.

As Kat watched her leave the house, she mused to herself, 'Tender sure is getting loose wit her lips. I don't know who the fuck she think she is? She better recognize. I will hurt her. She gettin' out of the pocket, comin' out her face sideways. She ain't been talkin' ta me like dat. And we ain't gonna start now. She got one more time ta say some slick shit. You heard! Then I'ma give her what she askin' for. A serious ass kickin' . . . You, bum bitch, I taught you everythin' you know. I put ya ass under my wing and showed you how to eat. Me! I gave you class. I gave you style. I gave you taste. Introduced you to things you never had or heard of. Yeah, me! I'm dat bitch! You owe me. And you 'bout ta pay like you owe me!"

Heading out the front door, Tender was oblivious to what was going on in Kat's head. She was greeted by a brand-new, platinum BMW 745, sitting on chrome, two-piece, twenty-two-inch rims. The car sparkled under the streetlights. Q sat in the driver's seat, nodding his head, banging a rap tune. Tender was an amateur car buff; she knew this car probably set him back about seventy to eighty thousand dollars. He was driving around in house money. Tender was glad that he didn't have tinted windows because this was definitely the type of car she wanted to be seen in. Besides that, if this was her car and she paid all that money for it, you were going to see her in living color.

Q watched Tender stroll. Her jeans were so tight, it looked like they were painted on. Boy, she got a helluva body on her. She'd make an old man wish for his younger years, he thought. The closer she got to the car, the more her face came into focus. Momentarily, Q studied it. He then realized she wasn't lacking in that department either. Without any makeup on she still looked good, a natural beauty.

"Q!" She squealed like a young girl as she entered the car.

He just shook his head as he watched her butt slowly fall into the seat. He couldn't help but lust. He couldn't help but reminisce over their last sexual encounter. He couldn't help himself from wanting to create more memories.

"Whew. God damn," he sighed. "What you do ta me?"

"Pleazzze! You tryin' ta run game on me." She flirted, giving him the goo-goo eyes. "Like you ain't neva seen me before . . . Tell dat ta sumbody else . . . Where we headed to?"

"Let's go out ta eat," he suggested. "I'm hungrier than a hostage."

"Where?" she replied. "You got someplace in mind?"

"Naw, not really. Fuck it. We can go ta Houston's. It's decent. A different type of atmosphere in there. No Thugs Allowed. We ain't gotta wear no bulletproof vests or eat wit a Tech Nine on da table. It's different from da other joints you usta eatin' at," he cracked, making fun of her.

"You got jokes, huh?" Tender shot back, laughing it off. "Ha, ha! Very funny . . ."

"Dis ain't a joke . . . Buckle up! You know what it is! Houston, we have ignition," he remarked, before taking off like a rocket.

Q had only been joking, but he spoke a little bit of truth, even in jest. Houston's was unlike any restaurant Tender had ever been to. She was use to frequenting McDonald's or Burger King, fast-food joints. The kind in the hood, that was strictly carry out, you couldn't even sit. This was a classy restaurant, she noted as they took their seats at a table for two. It was a totally different ball game. The lighting, setting, tables, chairs, the people and the conversations were different.

". . . President Bush should just drop a nuclear bomb on that whole damn country. They're all a bunch of terrorists, anyway . . ."

". . . Couldn't agree more with you, Skip. Our tax dollars help build up their economy. And this is how they repay us? . . ."

". . . After the company downsized. I received a nice severance package. I was able to roll that over . . ."

". . . Here's the trick when investing in Tech stocks. You have to know . . ."

From every which way, Tender's ears were bombarded by foreign conversation. She couldn't help but laugh to herself. If she had her eyes closed she would have sworn the speakers were of another ethnic origin. She was dining among society's movers and shakers. She was just a naive ghetto girl.

Had Q not been there, she would have felt out of place. This was a culture shock to her. Q watched closely as she faded in and out of their conversation. He could tell she was sensitive to and a bit uncomfortable to this mix. Q, on the other hand, was comfortable. He refused to conform to any ritzy dining dress code. He reflected what he was: the streets. Jeans, sneakers, boots, sweat suits were his attire. This was him, every day, all day. He had taken a page from the successful black CEO of Def Jam recordings, Russell Simmons's book. He made corporate America accept him, as is.

"You aiight?" he asked.

"Yeah, yeah, I'm good," she replied meekly. "Why you ask?"

He chuckled, "Why I ask, huh? I've been over here carryin' a conversation by myself fa da last five minutes. You been at every table, in every conversation except ours . . . You in everything but a good man's arms . . ."

"Fa real?" Tender asked, second-guessing him. "It wasn't dat bad? Wuz it?"

"You don't know?" he shot back. "If it get's any worst, you'll be sittin' here by yaself . . . Jus' kiddin! But anyway, what do you wanna eat? I'm tired a dis salad shit. I ain't no fuckin' rabbit. I want some meat, fish, chicken, sumthin'. I'm hungrier than I don't know what. . . ."

Tender stared at the menu. She could hardly make out the names of the dishes. It wasn't because she couldn't read. She could do that very well. The names were all funny-sounding. She didn't know how to pronounce these dishes, let alone order them. She pretended to be deep in thought, undecided on what to get. Every time Q glanced over at her, she strained her face like she was concentrating. He knew she was like a fish out of water in here, out of her element. He also knew Tender was too proud to ask for his help. He got that vibe from her, almost from the moment they met. Tender was a loner, an independent person. Whenever possible, she did for herself. She didn't depend on anybody. And especially no man.

Suddenly the waitress appeared. "Hi. How are y'all doin' this evening? Are ya'll ready to place your order? Ma'am? Sir?"

"You go, Q," Tender insisted. "I haven't decided yet."

"Dat's cool wit me," he commented. "As hungry as I am, I could eat anything cooked except pork. They'll be no swinin' and dinin' over here. Lips dat touch swine shall not touch mine . . ."

"Q! Aiight! Enuff iz enuff. We get da picture."

"I wuz jus sayin' . . ." He continued to joke. "But as long as I make myself perfectly clear . . . I'll be havin' filet mignon. Well done."

"What kind of vegetables would you like with that, sir?" the waitress asked. "We have fresh green peas, corn, green beans, spinach—"

"Lemme get a sucka shotta dat corn," he replied.

"And you, ma'am?" the waitress asked Tender.

Tender was stuck; she wasn't too fond of red meat but she didn't know how to decode the rest of the menu. All this fancy-dancy food—Q could have taken her to Mickey Dee's for this hassle. Suddenly she recalled a line from some old black-and-white movie she had been watching not too long ago. The line was kind of jazzy to her too. Now was the perfect time to use it.

"I'll have what he's havin,' " she said coolly.

"Now, dat wuz real original," he kidded her. "Did you think of dat all by yaself?"

"Shut up!" she fired back. "You get me sick. . . ."

Q laughed along with Tender. Deep down, he knew that he was making her day. And that she was feeling him. One of the things he dug about her was, he could say almost anything out of his mouth and nothing seemed to offend her. She took every-thing in stride and blew nothing out of proportion. If anything, she came back at him with a one-liner of her own. Armed with the knowledge that almost nothing offended her, and what she did for a living, Q decided to try his hand. He was about to ask her to do him a big favor. He'd definitely make it worth her while, by compensating her with cash.

Dinner was served, and their meal was delicious. Just as Tender's taste buds were getting accustomed to the seasoning of the food, it was gone. Now she knew why he frequented this restaurant; the food wasn't bad at all.

Besides the food, Tender thought Q looked edible. She wouldn't mind sinking her teeth into him, she thought. His braids really turned her on. She'd love to one day do them herself, she told him before. Just for the pleasure of running her fingers through his hair. Though he had an idea, Tender didn't really think how much he knew she was feeling him. How wet he got her. How she longed for him.

"Dig, Tee," he began, laying down his rap. "listen at me fa a second. I'm throw dis hypothetical question at you. Before you answer, give it some thought. Let it marinate in ya brain fa a li'l while. Let it bounce off da walls before you try ta catch it. . . ."

"Must you be so dramatic? Jus' skip da bull. And let me have it," she complained.

"See, dat's what I'm talkin' 'bout? Hush up when a playa iz rappin'," he joked. "Now where was I? . . . Oh, yeah . . . you listenin'? . . ."

"Yeah, ga 'head," she replied, anxious to hear what he had to say.

"If you had a significant otha. What I mean by dat iz, boyfriend, mate, booty call or whateva you wanna call 'im, and you wuz really, really, really feelin' dat cat, then to what extremes would you go ta please him?? Would you go da whole nine yards or stop at eight? Would you do anything and everything within ya woman duties ta see to it dat dis man wuz sexually satisfied? Or would he have to look elsewhere fa fulfillment? . . ." He went on spreading his rhetoric.

He continued. ". . . If you wuz really feelin' 'im like you claim, would you do da damn thang?"

Without a moment's hesitation she spoke, knowing that he was indirectly talking to her. And the two people in question were them.

"If I'm really feelin' 'im, and it's all like dat, then I'm gonna move out fa him. I'ma break him off whateva it iz he wants. I'ma please him, so he don't stray. He gone get everything he needs at home."

Though she was young in years, Tender knew that the fastest way to a man's heart wasn't through his stomach. It was keeping him satisfied in the bedroom. Fulfill his wildest fantasy and you got him. Every man wants his woman to be a lady in public and a slut behind closed doors. That was an undeniable fact. When one woman won't, one will. And if you're the I-Don't-Do-That-Type, then you would lose your man every time. An unhappy man will stray in a heartbeat.

It took every inch of self-restraint for Q to hide his excitement. From the sounds of things it's about to be on, he figured.

"Da reason I asked you dat iz . . ." He whispered as if he were confiding a secret with her. ". . . 'cause since I met you, I been havin' these dreams, fantasies 'bout you—"

Tender raised her brow, "What kinda dreams? You some kinda freak? You don't want me ta pee on you or nuttin'? Right? 'Cause, whoa . . . Lemme find out—"

"Naw, listen, dis iz serious bizness," he suggested. "Can I finish? Damn! . . . Anyway, like *I wuz sayin'*, I been havin' these fantasies 'bout me, you and . . . you know a ménage à trois . . . a

threesome . . . You ever did dat before? I ain't tryin' ta say ya . . .
Or nuttin' like dat. I'm jus askin', Na'mean? Neva hurt ta ask."

"No," she admitted. "Neva done dat. Hasn't even crossed my
mind . . ."

"No? . . ." he repeated. Her answer left him somewhat stuck.
Though Tender had never given him the impression that she was
Ms. Innocent, he could tell that she was kind of trying to angle toward being his girl. But this could never be. He already ruled that
out. Q could be extremely jealous at times. He didn't like sharing
his women with no other man. But on the other hand, he thought
variety was the spice of life. And when a stripper stripped, they
bared their bodies to other men. He couldn't live with that fact.
Just to think another man touched or lusted off his woman drove
him crazy. Though he acted as if he totally accepted Tender for
who she was and what she did, he secretly held it against her. The
fact that Tender was not or could not ever be his main squeeze let
him accept what she did for a living. He could have his cake and
eat it too—freaky sex.

"Lemme get dis right. You want me, and someone else, ta
freak wit you? Male or female?" she probed.

"Female, of course," Q quickly responded. "I don't wanna be
accidentally touchin' dicks wit nobody . . . Na'mean?"

A ménage à trois was every man's fantasy, Tender had been
told. Every man wanted the experience—at least once in his lifetime—before marriage or death. Now here she was, being
propositioned by a very powerful man. She wasn't repulsed or
turned off by the idea of having sex and sharing Q with another
woman. In fact, she was a little curious. Hey, you can't knock it till
you try it, she always thought. If this was her way in, if this is
what would make him happy, so be it. She figured she'd score
some points with him and position herself closer to him. If she
couldn't be his number one, then she would settle for being his
mistress. She figured to reap the rewards as such. After all, one

hand washes the other but they both wash the face. A favor for a favor.

Q tried to laugh off her comment. "Why you gotta say it like dat?"

"C'mon, now. It is what it is. Stop beatin' around da bush . . . It's all good. Count me in," she boldly stated.

"Dat's what's up!" he said, applauding her decision. "I knew you'd ride fa a nigga. Tender, you's one down-ass broad. You keeps it real all da way 'round da board . . ."

Yeah, whatever! Tender thought. She saw the big picture. Getting with Q offered something that she didn't have, financial stability.

"Listen, I ain't do dis wit any bitch!" Tender warned. "I gotta personally approve of her. She gotta be clean, attractive, with no foul body odor—"

"Matter fact, you get her," he said, trying to be funny.

"Aiight, I will," she replied seriously.

"However you wanna do it, dat's cool wit me . . . Whatever makes you comfortable," he suggested. "Just be ready ta do da damn thang, da day afta tomorrow. . . ."

The day after tomorrow came so fast, Tender didn't have adequate time to be as selective as she liked. The few girls she thought about approaching, either she couldn't catch up with them or they were on their monthly cycle. Either way, she was in a jam. She was on the clock and pressed to produce another participant. She looked high and low to no avail. Then finally she turned to Kat as a last resort.

Kat tried to play hard to get. But this was only a front to hide her joy. Wild horses couldn't drag her away from this. The money she was given by Tender, from Q, was icing on the cake. She would have done it for nothing—just for the cause; because he was who he was.

If Q did something, he always made sure he did it right. He

spared no expense when it came time to fulfill his sexual fantasy. He rented a suite in a five-star hotel in downtown Philly. Tender was given a handsome allowance of five thousand dollars to do what she had to do on her end. Q was no cheapskate; he knew you had to pay to play.

Though Tender wasn't all for Kat being in on this, she went along with the program. From her statements in the past, she knew Kat was freaky enough to do it. She still wondered to this day if Kat ever went down on another girl before. Knowing her, she didn't put it past her. There was no turning back now; everything had to go as planned, or she ran the risk of losing Q. Surely, a man of his stature had females scattered across the city at his beck and call.

"Listen, I'ma give you some more money toward dat lawyer fa Goldie," Tender stated. "Put dat wit the other money you had fa me. From Miami?"

"Oh, . . ." she replied, somewhat puzzled before catching on. "Alright. I gotcha. If we hustle a little harder we should have enuff to hire her the best lawyer in the city. She needs a good trial lawyer. Not only who's gonna get her to cop out ta an asshole fulla time."

Little did Tender know, she wasn't contributing any money toward hiring a lawyer for Goldie. She was donating her money to the Keep Kat Living It Up Fund. And there would be no refunds.

"I know," Tender assured her. "Them muthafucka's iz expensive as shit too."

"Yeah, they sure don't work fa peanuts," Kat added. "But we can do it. We gotta do it fa our girl. We da only hope she's got—"

"You right about dat," Tender admitted. "You heard from her lately? I think I missed her call."

"Yeah, she called while you were 'sleep," Kat lied. "She doin' betta. My peoples iz takin' care of her. They lookin' out fa her.

She's in good hands . . . I told her just ta keep her head up. Na'mean? She'll be back in Philly inna minute."

Kat was lying out the side of her mouth. She hadn't heard from Goldie since she left. Having changed her house telephone number, it would almost be impossible for Goldie to call. Her cell phone number remained the same, only because she had loyal customers on it. Even if she did call, Kat would probably hang up the phone on her. She wanted no contact with her. Goldie was hot; she was wanted by the cops. Kat didn't want that kind of heat around her. Let Goldie stay where she was at. She hoped Goldie would do everybody a favor and just kill herself.

"C'mon, da limo's here," Tender announced, peeking out the living room window.

They took a trip to the hotel in style. Q had provided them with a rented canary yellow stretch Hummer. Silently they sat like assassins, contemplating what they were about to do. Kat even went so far as to visualize how it would all go down. She planned on being three things—nasty, aggressive and greedy. That was the only way she thought she could leave her mark, a lasting sexual impression.

Tender, on the other hand, wondered how the chips would fall. She had only heard stories about threesomes. She never actually witnessed one or had been involved in one. She was doing this for the wrong reasons—to please a man, not to satisfy her own wild side.

One minute they were leaving the house, and the next, they were pulling up in front of the hotel—the time seemed to fly. The driver quickly exited the car to open the door for his passengers. The girls filed out in identical black Burberry raincoats with matching black stiletto boots on. Large oval Gucci shades covered their eyes, almost hiding their faces. Underneath the raincoats they were both naked as newborn babies.

As they strutted through the hotel lobby, the outlines of their curvaceous bodies could be seen, as the raincoats clung to their skin. They oozed with sex appeal, attracting the attention of many male admirers.

Once on the elevator, Tender pushed the button for the seventh floor. Stepping back as the door closed, she couldn't help but notice how roomy the elevator was. The ones around the way or in the projects were always so small, cramped, crowded and sometimes reeked of urine. Coming to an abrupt halt, the elevator reached it's designated floor, depositing the girls. It was showtime.

They both walked confidently toward suite 705. Out the corner of her eye Tender snuck quick peeks at Kat. She wondered what was running through her mind. She was unsure what to expect behind this door. But looking at her, you would have never known it. Unnoticed, they passed by a group of maids as they performed their jobs of straightening up the rooms. Producing a credit card type key from her coat pocket, Tender inserted it into the slot. A green light came on, unlocking the door.

The first thing they noticed was how dimly lit the room was. Scented candles, strategically placed, provided the only light they would need. The curtains were closed, giving anyone in the room a false sense of the time of day. As instructed, the girls followed a trail of red rose petals that led straight to the king-sized canopy bed. The closer they got, a strong scent of marijuana began to fill their nostrils. As they walked through the living room and entered the bedroom, they saw huge billows of smoke floating in the air and the bright orange ash glow from the tip of a lit joint. Q sat in the corner puffing on a blunt. He watched as they entered the room.

The purple haze marijuana Q smoked was powerful. He was an avid weed smoker; he could handle it. The euphoric feeling that came over him made him horny, freaky to be exact. This was his Viagra, Ecstasy, his love drug. There would be no premature

ejaculation while he was high off this. He planned on going long
and strong. Not that he really needed it anyway. It was more of a
psychological thing. It was a confidence booster.

"Ladies," he greeted them, in a deep seductive tone. Through
squinted eyes, he strained trying to size up the girls. Sis look
good, he thought, referring to Kat. He was already fully aroused.
There was something about new pussy that excited him. It always
made him come back for seconds. He often wondered was it really good or was it just his imagination. Q never ascribed to the
theory, "It's never as good as the first time." He knew he was
going to enjoy being in the middle of this man sandwich. Little
ole him, blanketed by two gorgeous girls.

The girls proceeded to undo their raincoats, letting them fall
to their feet, exposing their well-sculpted bodies. Tender went
and retrieved a bottle of baby oil from a nearby table. After
squeezing out a handful of the lubricant, she passed it to Kat,
who did the same. All of this was done in complete silence. This
was part of their role-playing.

Facing each other, they took turns gently massaging the baby
oil into each other's skin. Working her way down Kat's body, Tender felt sort of strange. Though she had seen plenty of naked
women working in the club, she never touched another woman's
body, not in this fashion, nor did she have any desire to. She was
amazed at the difference in feel from a man's body. The hardness
and roughness of a man's muscles and skin were absent, replaced
by a soft elasticity and smoothness that only a woman possessed.
A woman's body should have come with instructions to handle
with care. She rubbed Kat down carefully, avoiding going anywhere near her genitals. That wasn't something she wanted to
touch, she wasn't gay or curious. Anything that bled and didn't
die, she didn't want in her mouth.

When that was done, it was Kat's turn to play masseuse. She
really was into it. Her touch was notably different. Tender picked

up on it right away. There was something provocative, sexually suggestive, about the motion of her hands. It felt like she was being caressed by a lover. Methodically, Kat cupped, brushed and ran her fingertips along Tender's body, giving her goose bumps. As hard as she tried to fight the feeling, she hated to admit it, but it felt good. Tender felt as though she could close her eyes and be carried away by a warm tropical ocean current. Then a finger, by accident, mistake or on purpose managed to touch her vagina. This caused her to snap back to reality and jump back. She shot Kat a perplexed look that said, "What you doin'? What part of the game is that? Don't go there." Kat never said a word, she just smirked at her devilishly.

Moving along with the show, the girls took off their boots, and got on the bed. Then they pretended to wrestle each other. The whole scene was choreographed, rehearsed for Q's enjoyment. And boy did he ever enjoy. He got a kick out of seeing them go at it. He always was a big wrestling fan, particularly of women wrestlers. But on TV they didn't get raw like this. Buttocks and breasts were everywhere. First Tender was on top, fighting against fake resistance. Then they flip-flopped positions. They tussled and gently pulled each other's hair. This went on for a couple of minutes before Q decided to finish his blunt and join in.

Like octopuses, arms, legs and tongues seemed to be everywhere. Q was in the middle of the excitement, receiving a tongue bath. The girls divided him in half, with Tender taking the upper body and Kat focusing on the lower. Kat went straight for his manhood, taking it in her mouth. She spit on it and then licked it clean. She repeated the process numerous times. Meanwhile, Tender lovingly held Q's face in her hands, while their tongues swam violently in each other's mouths. He eagerly matched her passion with equal parts of his own.

As Kat furiously bobbed her head up and down, she snuck a peek up at Q and Tender. And even though she was doing a hell of a job, it seemed like Tender had his undivided attention. In an attempt to steal the show, Kat moved from his penis to his scrotum, before licking hungrily at his anus. She had her own agenda, to be as freaky as she could. If she had her way, this would be Tender's last time with Q. Before he knew it, she had his legs spread in the air while she attacked his asshole like there was no tomorrow.

"*OOOOO*hhh!!" he moaned, finally breaking his lip lock. "SSSSSssss . . ."

Previously, his asshole had been no man's land. Never in his life had he had a woman freak him like this. Through facial expressions, he begged her to stop. But his mouth didn't move to ennunciate the words. Somehow, they were stuck in his throat.

Tender couldn't believe what Kat was doing. This bitch is nasty, she thought. There was no way in the world she was doing that. There was nothing anybody could say to convince her otherwise.

Finally, Q had had enough, he broke Kat's beastly grip, bringing his legs to a rest on the bed. Though the sensation was good, unlike anything he'd ever experienced sexually, the position in which he was placed wasn't masculine at all. That was reason enough for him to stop it. His ego was killing him. He wondered, What would his friends think if they could see him?

Clearly, Kat was the aggressor here. Tender had fallen back somewhat, giving her room to work. She licked from his scrotum upward, leaving a trail of saliva till she found the opening of his mouth. They exchanged sloppy French kisses, to Tender's amazement. Then Kat scooted her body up, and sat on his face. Q helped himself to an endless amount of her love juices. He was barely able to breathe. His nose and mouth seemed to be buried inside her vagina. Like dogs in heat, they seemed to go at it.

Tender managed to get back into the mix of things, but it wasn't the same. It seemed as if Q was more into Kat than her.

She was beginning to feel left out. Even when he wasn't having sex with Kat, he was touching, kissing, feeling and talking dirty to her. Tender never factored this possibility into the equation when she agreed to this ménage à trois. If this had crossed her mind, she would never have done it. He would have had to find someone else. Not her. She felt betrayed by him. This is the thanks I get for "ridin" for him? she thought.

# 13

GOLDIE BOARDED an Amtrack express train at the Market Street station in Philadelphia. Nervously, Goldie looked around suspiciously at the other passengers. Everyone appeared to be an undercover cop to her. That's how paranoid she was. She felt as though she were walking on eggshells, as if her every move was being watched. She thought at any given moment the law would spring from the shadows and haul her off to jail. This caused her to stop in her tracks many times, as travelers suddenly shifted directions, on her way to board a train. Needless to say, her schizophrenic actions drew more attention to her than anything else.

She breathed a big sigh of relief when the train finally departed. Goldie could run from her problems but she couldn't hide. The demons that troubled her soul were going along on this trip with her, just like the luggage she carried. Her eyes were glued outside the window. She took one last look at her city, the only home she ever knew, and silently bid it farewell. She was leaving and doubted if she'd ever return.

New York, New York, big city of dreams. That phrase came to mind as Goldie headed for the city. She managed to get out of Philadelphia without getting arrested by Philadelphia's finest. Still, she wasn't so sure how long her luck would hold up.

Arriving at Penn Station, Goldie gathered her luggage and exited the train. She followed the crowd of people up the escalator, unsure of which direction to go. Subconsciously, she had grown so dependent on Kat to make decisions for her that she was lost on her own. It took her a while to realize that there was no one around to lead her. No one around to help weather this emotional storm. No one to help her through these gloomy rainy days of this thing called life. She was in a sink-or-swim situation. She had to fend for herself. Only time would tell if she would make it.

The mass of people that shuffled through Penn Station amazed her. They all seemed to be in a hurry. Goldie tried to stop a few people to ask for some directions, but they ignored her. The residents of New York were mean, and some downright nasty. To her they all seemed to have a chip on their shoulder, an attitude. She could relate to the New York state of mind. Native New Yorkers had to adopt certain mannerisms in order to survive. The Big Apple that out-of-towners saw on TV was not the place they knew. The city was cruel, so they had to be crueler. Every day brought the possibility of a new threat, and every stranger was potentially dangerous.

After a few frustrating hours, Goldie finally devised a plan. She bought a city paper and looked in the classified section for furnished rooms for rent. It didn't matter to her what part of the city she stayed in, since she'd never been here anyway. The cheapest room she could find determined where she would rest her head. She came across an ad for a furnished room in Mount Vernon. That's where she was headed; only problem was how she was going to get there.

"Excuse me, officer," she said, stopping a Port Authority cop.

"I'm a little lost. See, I'm not from New York. I'm here visiting some relatives . . . And they were supposed to meet me here, and they're nowhere to be found . . . I was wondering, can you tell me how ta get ta Mount Vernon? How much would it cost me to go by cab?"

Mount Vernon was a section of Westchester County, which was located at the northernmost tip of the borough of The Bronx. At certain points, a city block was all that separated the two.

"Miss, I wouldn't suggest that you take a cab from downtown Manhattan way up to Mount Vernon. That'll cost you a pretty penny. Do you know how far that is?" he stated. "If I were you, and I couldn't get in contact with any friends or family, I'd take the number two train, north. Ride it to the last stop. That'll take you to 242nd Street. From there, you can walk a few blocks to Mount Vernon or catch a cab. You're right there."

"Where do I find dis . . . number two train?" she asked innocently. "And how much does it cost?"

"Walk down this corridor," the policeman began. "Make a sharp left. Keep walkin' straight and you'll run right into it. And it only costs two dollars . . . One thing about New York, the subway runs all night long. And it'll take you to or near anywhere you wanna go in the five boroughs . . . Remember that . . . Or else you'll spend a fortune on cabs . . . Cabdrivers are rip-off artists. Somebody like you, who doesn't know the city, they'll take on the scenic route . . ."

"Thanks for the advice, officer," she remarked.

GOLDIE TUSSLED WITH HER LUGGAGE as she walked through the long corridor. People watched her struggle; no one offered to lend a hand. She was already off to a bad start. If this was any indication of her stay in the city, then things were going to be rough.

She followed the directions to a *T*. Standing on the subway platform, she pressed her back against a steel support beam. She didn't want to let anyone slip behind her, and push her in front of an oncoming train. She saw the horror stories on the news about things like that happening. She didn't fear dying; Goldie just didn't want to die a painful death like that.

New York City's transit system was one of the biggest in the nation. So the trains came like clockwork to handle the millions of people who commuted to and from work every day. Goldie's wait was short. She heard and felt the rumbling of the platform. This was her signal that the train was coming. She took a quick glance behind her, making sure the coast was clear, and then she leaned her head and neck close to the edge of the platform, peeking into the pitch black tunnel, trying to spot the train. There it was speeding toward her. The train's white headlights shone through the blackness. Atop the train, she could see a luminescent circular number 2. "This must be my train," she told herself. Then she went and collected her belongings.

The train rumbled into the 34th Street station, bringing with it a thunderous, almost ear-piercing noise. Goldie was almost knocked down as mobs of people exited the train in a rush. She managed to fight her way through just to enter. She found an empty seat as soon as she got on. There were plenty of empty seats around her. But for some reason everyone in the car was crowded and bunched up at the other end. As she settled in her seat, it hit her—an odor so strong, it was sickening. She spotted a dirty black homeless man curled up in a seat, fast asleep. His hair was extremely nappy. His face and clothes were so dirty, it looked as if he worked in the shaft of a coal mine. At the very next stop, she got up and moved too. She stood up at the other end for the rest of the ride.

Her ride through the underground subway tunnels and to high elevated tracks ended an hour and a half later, at 241st Street. Once again, she struggled with her luggage. But a Good

Samaritan finally came to her aid. He helped her down the flight of stairs to the street, where she hopped into a gypsy cab. She gave him the address and he drove her there. The rooming house was no more than a converted private house. On the outside, it looked nice. Goldie hoped the same could be said for the inside. She kept her fingers crossed.

Goldie looked at the classified ad one more time, just to be sure she was at the right place. Things seemed to be in order, so she rang the bell.

"Who iz it?" a woman's voice demanded to know, from behind the front door.

"My name iz . . ." she began, "Gloria. I saw ya ad in da paper about a room for rent. And I came over ta check it out . . ."

With that said, she began to hear the sound of the door unlocking.

The door swung open and there stood a small, black, mean-looking old lady.

"This must be ya lucky day," the woman commented. "I just had to evict one a my tenants not too long ago . . . I was just cleaning up the room now . . . You wouldn't believe how some people live. He was a nasty son of a gun—"

"So, you do have a room available?" she inquired.

"Sure do," the old woman replied. "But I don't take in just any ole body. The last time I did that . . . Boy! I was too nice . . ." She was the owner of the property; she owned it but didn't live there. She had another house around the corner, where she stayed. Often, she would drop by on the spur of the moment to check up on her tenants. At one time, she only came by once a week to collect the rent, until things got out of hand. One of her borders had turned the rooming house into a full-fledged crack house. Ever since then, she's been popping up at all times of the day and night. She cleaned house, throwing out all the deadbeats and undesirables.

"Listen, young lady. There are rules in this here house. And if you're not good at following rules, ain't no sense in you comin' in."

"I can follow rules, ma'am," she stated with a hint of desperation in her voice. "I won't be no trouble, no trouble at all . . . I don't bother nobody . . . I stay ta myself . . . You won't even know I'm here."

"I heard that before," the old woman said sarcastically as she scrutinized the person in front of her. Usually she was a good judge of character.

"I promise, ma'am, you will not have no trouble outta me," Goldie reiterated.

"Alright, you can have the room," the old woman said. "You seem like a good person. But let me tell you somethin'. Don't you be havin' all kind of strange men runnin' in and outta here at all times of the night. You're only allowed one, maybe two, people at the most up in your room at a time. I got six rooms in here. If all my tenants had a lot of company, then it's problems. Things get missin' and my property get toe' up! I worked too damn hard to let someone else destroy my house. You know what I mean? Anyway, I'll need a hundred-dollar security deposit. Plus two weeks' rent, up front . . ."

Third street was the name of the block Goldie now lived on. In Mount Vernon, this was as ghetto as it got. It was just as barren and bleak as her old neighborhood in Philly, just on a smaller scale. Here people, young and old, hung out on the avenue, signifying, drinking, smoking and selling drugs. This was the usual madness that went on in almost any minority community. It was Goldie's home now, till the heat died down. When that would be there was no telling. For her sake, it had better be soon. She was thrown back into the same drug-plagued, negative environment she grew up in. Temptations, as well as her ghosts, were all around her. She was psychologically scarred. In her frame of mind, she was a disaster waiting to happen. Goldie was in the fight of her life, for her life.

Her room was small and cramped, but clean. The only things in it were a twin bed, small closet, night table, an old black-and-white TV, which sat atop a brown wooden beat-up dresser. She hadn't seen one of these things in years. She wondered if they still made them. As long as the place was clean, it didn't bother her that she didn't have any of the comforts of home. She didn't care about cable TV, DVDs or VCRs. She wasn't really into them like that. She relished the fact that this room didn't have all these electronic appliances. She welcomed the solitude and tranquillity that the house offered. Maybe now she could get her mind right. If anything, she was going to buy a radio so she could listen to some church music to hear God's word day and night. That would be more than enough entertainment for her.

The only thing she didn't really like about the place was sharing space with the other tenants. Specifically, the kitchen and bathroom was the cause of her concern. She knew everyone was not clean. People leave behind some despicable things in bathrooms and there was a possibility that someone could steal her food, if it was left in the refrigerator. These were some of the things that she would have to deal with, like it or not.

Goldie unpacked her things. She neatly folded up all her clothes that she couldn't hang in the closet, placing them in the dresser drawers. She placed the phone number Kat gave her on her night table. She didn't plan on calling it just yet. But she wanted to keep it within reach, so she didn't lose it. Besides her friends, Tender's and Kat's cell phone numbers, this was her only lifeline. Then she removed her small black Bible and her ever-present diary. She needed to update her journal to the latest events. She had been too paranoid to do so on the train. Sitting on the edge of the bed, diary in her lap, pen in hand, she wrote feverishly, nonstop. She needed to release all her frustration and negative emotions that were built up inside of her. Soon after she finished writing, she curled up on the bed and drifted fast asleep.

". . . GLORIA, you look so pretty in your Easter dress," her mother said, beaming. "You look like one of God's angels . . . You are an angel. My little angel."

"Thank you, Mommy," she said, as she posed for an Easter picture in front of their building. "I get it from you . . . I get my looks from you."

Sound asleep, Goldie dreamed of happier times in her childhood. She reminisced about her Communion at St. Mary's Church and all the long walks in the park she and her mother had shared. The essence of the beautiful bond they had when she was a kid. How did that go so horribly wrong? She didn't have to search the inner crevices of her mind or the core of her soul for the answer. She already knew, but wouldn't admit it. All her problems began in her adolescence. The rift that divided them was Angel. Her relationship with him was to blame.

In one fateful day, the day her mother died, her world turned upside down. And even in her dream, Goldie began to cry. She regretted dearly what had happened to her mother. If there was a way to undo what was already done, she would. If there was a way she could take her mother's place, she would. If? If? If?

Even in dreamland, Goldie was unable to come to grips with what had happened. She woke up in a cold sweat. Immediately, she reached inside her purse and grabbed a brownish-looking medicine bottle. She unscrewed the top, took two pills out and placed them in her mouth. Using only saliva, she washed them down. Just the mere thought of how good they were going to make her feel lifted her spirits. She was happy to be escaping her own personal hell, however brief it was.

In the following weeks, desperation began to set in on Goldie. The money Kat had given her was just about gone. She spent her money on three things, eating out, feeding her drug habit and paying rent. She had no money coming in, so this was bound to happen. But Goldie never took that into account. Her mind was clouded by the drugs she was using. When she came to the realization that she didn't have any more drugs and was low on cash, she began to panic. She had to revert to the quickest way she knew to make good money, stripping.

She began to search the area for local strip clubs. As chance would have it, she came upon one of the most prominent strip clubs in New York City. One of the best on the whole entire East Coast. It was called Sue's Rendezvous. This club was world renowned for it's beautiful strippers. It boasted the best of the best, cream of the crop. Many strippers who thought they fit the bill soon learned otherwise. The club was very particular whom they let dance there. Because they had an A-list of celebrities who frequented the club on any given night, they couldn't afford to let some two-bit stripper ruin their business. So they reserved the right to be selective.

Goldie was a cutie; her body was still intact. She hadn't slipped that far, to where she neglected her looks. Sue's Rendezvous management was impressed by her looks. Being Hispanic was another thing in her favor. The club featured lots of beautiful Latino women. Goldie could hold her own in the beauty department against the best they had to offer. So fortunately for her, they liked her. They hired her on the spot.

Unlike most strip clubs, where the stripper had to resort to extreme measures for chump change, at Sue's Rendezvous, the patrons spoiled the girls. They lavished them with big bills. It was nothing to get a hundred dollars for a lap dance. Men literally sat at the bar with stacks of bills, handing them out to whoever caught their eye. It is safe to say these strippers were taken care of.

At the club, Goldie kept her distance from the other strippers. She didn't want to befriend anyone. They were strangers to her, as she was to them. It was all about money, the Benjamin's. She was there just to pay her rent and support her habit. After that, she went her way and they went theirs. What she did outside the club was nobody's business.

As the weeks went by, Goldie continued to strip. As her drug habit grew, she consumed more and more of a wide variety of drugs. They ranged from Ecstasy, Valiums, to mescaline tabs. Venturing out into her neighborhood, Goldie came in contact with some of the local junkies. They turned her on to all the drug spots in the area. When she wasn't stripping at the club, she was barracaded in her room doing drugs, getting as high as she could. This only amplified her state of depression. Alone in her room, she would replay the tragic events that surrounded her life. Over and over again she reflected, as if this were her favorite TV show. To Goldie, she was cursed, cursed by Murphy's Law, which stated, "Anything that can go wrong, will go wrong." Her horrifying thoughts were the only company she kept.

During this time, she began to experience terrible bouts of homesickness. She wondered what Tender was doing. What was taking them so long to send for her? She decided to reach out and call her. She rang the phone repeatedly, but got no reply. Tender had never set up her answering service, so she couldn't even leave a message. That's when she tried to call the house.

". . . The number you have dialed, two-one-five–five-five-five–four-three-seven-six, has been changed to an unlisted number. No further information is available," the automated voice said.

Goldie was crushed. She felt as if the world had abandoned her. Where were her friends during her time of need? She questioned, "Why did they change the number all of a sudden? Did they forget about me?"

Immediately after that, she phoned Kat. This was the last person in the world she wanted to talk to. But she really didn't have much of a choice. Who else could she call?

"Hello?" Kat spoke into the receiver. "Who dis?"

"It's me, Goldie," she said meekly. "I been tryin' ta get in contact with y'all. Who changed da number?"

"Listen," Kat barked. "don't be callin' here trippin' on me 'bout my muthafuckin' phone . . . You musta lost ya damn mind! Anyway, Tender had da phone number changed. Talk ta her 'bout dat . . ."

"She did?" Goldie asked in disbelief.

"Yeah, she did!" Kat insisted.

"Don't believe dat. She wouldn't do dat ta me. Dat's my girl . . ."

"Believe whatcha' wanna believe. You asked and I told you. Take it for what it's worth . . . She usta be ya girl . . . Tender's two-faced. She ain't got no love fa you. Da otha day, I asked her fa some money towards ya lawyer and she said she ain't got it. I ain't heard no more about it either . . . She sold you a dream."

In her emotionally unbalanced mind, depressed and delusional, Goldie actually began to believe this lie. She didn't give Tender the benefit of the doubt. Kat was so convincing, she gave the lie an air of authenticity. Never mind the fact she knew Kat was cruddy, at least she had the decency to answer her cell phone. She should have known better; after all, she knew Kat the longest. As many boldface lies she caught her in over the years, she knew from experience how cunning she was. Still, now that Kat said this to her, Tender's unwillingness to answer her phone was an automatic admission of guilt.

". . . Anyway, forget about her. You don't need her. I'ma hold you down. Aiight? Jus gimme a li'l more time and I promise I'll have dat dough fa ya lawyer," Kat said convincingly.

"How long iz dat?" Goldie pressed her for an answer. "I been

out here a month already. I wanna come home. I don't like it
here. New York ain't fa me."

"Don't you even think 'bout comin' back yet. Not here!" she
warned her sternly. ". . . Da police will be on you like stink on
shit. They watchin' the bus terminal, train station and airport.
They handin' out wanted flyers wit ya face on 'em. If I wuz you,
I'd stay my black ass right where I'm at. Ain't nuttin' worse than
gettin' caught, goin' ta jail, then goin' ta court wit a Public De-
fender. . . ."

A couple times, Kat almost gave herself away; she almost
burst out in laughter. Even she couldn't believe how good of a lie
she was telling. She spontaneously fabricated this story so well.
All Goldie had to do was connect the dots. Everything she said
would coincide. She succeeded in playing with her head.

"I don't know how much longer I can take dis," Goldie admitted. "Jus' hurry up and send fa me . . . Okay?"

"Aiight! I'm on my job," she stated, making an empty promise. "Did you call dat number I gave you?" Lemme get off dis
phone. I think it might be tapped. Talk ta ya later!"

"Not yet," Goldie replied.

"Do dat," Kat advised. "They my peoples, call 'em. They can
help you out. Put money in ya pocket. For da time bein' . . ."

Kat continued, "What wuz dat? You heard dat noise?"

"Where? What you talkin' 'bout?" she asked. "I ain't hear
nuttin'."

"Shhuusshh!" she whispered. ". . . There it go again! I think
my phone iz tapped. I'll talk ta ya later . . . Bye!!"

Just like that she was gone. Meanwhile, Goldie was left standing at the pay phone dumbfounded. Little did she know this
would be the last time she'd talk to Kat.

# 14

AFTER THE MÉNAGE À TROIS, Tender shied away from Kat. She'd given one hundred percent of herself to their friendship and in return all she got was Kat's ass to kiss. For her loyalty and devotion all she received was empty promises and a pack of lies. She questioned herself, how could she have been so gullible? How could she have put her life in Kat's hands?

Tender had a strange notion, that Q and Kat were seeing each other behind her back. She wasn't stressing out behind that though. She didn't like it, but what could she do. She didn't own him. He was free to do what he liked. After all, she was still sleeping with him and he was still taking care of her. She just wished they would be up front about it.

The whole situation was bigger than a man. She knew she made a mistake by bringing Kat around him. She rationalized, "Men come and go. Friends last forever." True friends do. They don't cross certain lines.

True to her word, Tender began to hustle up the money for Goldie's lawyer. She began spending as much time working as humanly possible. She spent as little time as possible at her so-called home. She only slept there. She and Kat began to see less and less of each other. That was because Kat was spending quite a lot of time out of the house herself, with Q.

"Tenda, c'mere! Come holla atcha gurl!" Luscious yelled across the somewhat empty club.

Luscious was an older stripper who Tender had gotten familiar with by dancing in the same clubs. There were quite a few strip joints in Philly, but when you travel in the same circles, you're bound to run into the same people. Plus their personalities were so much alike, laid back, that they couldn't help but to like each other.

"It's fuckin' dead in here tanite," Tender announced. "I shoulda stayed home! I ain't neva seen it like dis."

"Hey, get usta it," Luscious cautioned. "If you been around long as I have, you'll see. Every night ain't a good night. It be like dis sometime . . . I can remember me and my girlfriend sittin' at dis same bar, cryin' our eyes out it was so bad. . . . We went home da way we came in. Broke!!!"

"Damn! Well what did you do on days like dis?" Tender inquired. "How you make it?"

"I learned," she began. "It took me a while but I learned. Da name of da game iz adapt and adopt. You gotta adapt certain ways. And adopt certain things. . . . I started datin' and gettin' regular customers and on slow days I'd call 'em up. They'd come thru . . . Come thru like da Wu . . . deeper than da Wu-Tang Clan in dis bitch. Shit!"

"Wish you call 'em now," Tender stated. "Dis place could use da cash flow. Dis shit iz ridiculous. . . ."

"Now you know I can't turn you on ta my people," she joked. "Dey might fall in love wit dat young tight pussy you got. . . . Then dey won't wanna fuck wit a old hag like me . . . and you know dat's right!"

"Yeah, tell about it! Don't I know it!" Tender admitted. "I already been there and done that. I got da shirt and I ain't goin' back . . ."

"What you talkin' 'bout, young gurl?" she said playfully. "You don't know nuttin' 'bout dat . . ."

"Long story, you know. Drama! Sssoooo much drama," Tender replied. "Strippin' and bullshit . . . Who you callin' young girl anyway? Age ain't nuttin' butta number. I'm wise beyond my years—"

"I don't care whatcha say. You still my young buck!" she commented.

"And you my oldhead," Tender shot back.

"You jus' make it ta my age. You jus' make it there, . . ." she said confidently. "Shit, look at me. I'm damn near forty years old. Wit da body and face of a twenty-year-old . . ."

Tender was surprised by this admission. She knew her counterpart was older, but not that much older. What was she still doing in the game? Even with a hell of a body. Shouldn't she be already situated in her life? Shouldn't she have already settled down? she mused.

"Damn, Luscious," she said. "I didn't know you was dat old, girl."

"Why, 'cause I talk dat talk, huh? . . ." she commented.

"Naw, 'cause you don't look a day over twenty-five," Tender said, stroking her ego.

"Thanks . . . but look at me . . . I'm still doin' da same ole shit afta all these years . . . I been doin' dis shit fa so long . . . I think I'm fuckin' soma my customers' son's . . . No bullshittin' . . . I 'member when I wuz a wide-eye rookie like you. I wuz green as grass . . ."

Her voice began to crack and Tender swore she saw a tear in her eye. Her mood had switched from jolly to sad. She looked at Tender; she saw herself. She saw all the potential she once possessed. She never finished school. She never did anything she said she was going to do. Luscious had gotten sidetracked and now she was stuck. She was an old woman in a young woman's game. She was growing more desperate by the day.

"How did you start strippin'?" Tender asked. "I mean why? . . ."

Luscious paused, and then cleared her throat. "I had to . . . see, my mother wuz in a bad car crash. She laid up in da hospital fa a while. She was on and off life support. Befo' she died, I made a promise ta her ta take care of my li'l sister and my li'l brother. I found out 'bout dis and I been doin' eva since. . . ."

"But didn't make enuff ta take care of them? How old are dey right now?"

"Of course I made enuff . . . I took care a them. Put 'em through private school . . . They grown now wit kids of they own . . . I don't even think they realize the sacrifice I made for them . . . Na'mean? . . . I kept tellin' myself one day I wuz gonna quit. One day I wuz gonna stop . . . You know what, that day neva came yet! . . . I'm still here . . . Afta all these years . . . Tender, I'm tellin' you some good shit. Don't be like me . . . Use da game as a stepping-stone. Or it'll use you. It'll eat you alive, take da best years of ya life . . . Do what you gotta do. Just know you gotta change . . . Don't be like me . . . Make it out da game fo' it's too late. . . ."

Suddenly, Tender remembered how Kat's sister, Jackie, tried to warn her in the beginning. She didn't listen then because she didn't know any better. She didn't believe her, but maybe she should have.

TENDER WAS READY to get out of the stripping game now. The conversation she had with Luscious spoke volumes to her soul. She saw that material possessions weren't worth losing her life. She was worth more than that.

As it was, though, she wasn't rich; she wasn't broke either. How much money was enough? Or would it never be enough? It was time to cut her losses and move on. She made plans to make her escape. Maybe she'd join Goldie in New York. That would be nice, she thought.

"WHAT AM I DOIN' HERE?" Tender asked herself, dressed in black, shiny, latexlike trench coat with matching stiletto pumps. Armed with handcuffs, ropes and a whip, she looked like a black villain for some comic book. But this was no joke. What she was about to do was real; the last money that she'd make in this game.

The scent of money had recently led her to some of the strip clubs frequented by white businessmen. Before she would have avoided them because it was such a culture shock to her. But truth be told this was where the "real" money was. But the more money she was given, the weirder the sexual perversion became. She was asked to do some very strange things.

Her date tonight was with Marvin, a short, white, hairy, pot-bellied guy. He was a prominent businessman at a major pharmaceutical company. He had a fetish for leather, whips, chains and black women. The combination aroused him more than sexual intercourse itself. He spent thousands of dollars a week with Tender just to be beaten.

He always paid up front. Marvin even paid for the hotel. They arranged to meet in Bucks County, just outside of the city of Philadelphia, at the Ramada Inn. He took this precaution out of fear of being spotted with a black woman, entering or leaving the hotel, by his family or colleagues. He would never be able to explain that.

He possessed a split personality, like Jekyll and Hyde, pretending to be one way in public, another behind closed doors.

Tender was repulsed at the sight of him. She fed right into that old stereotype that said white people smelled like dogs. It was a myth that most black people really believed. Marvin's stench came from releasing his bowels while Tender beat the living daylights out of him.

"Marvin, you been a bad boy? Haven't you?" she asked, playing the role of a dominatrix.

"Yeah, I been a bad boy," he said, in a childlike voice. "I didn't do my homework . . . the teacher caught me talking to my best bud in class . . . and I broke my glasses . . . on purpose. . . ."

"Oh, you a real Billy Bad-Ass, huh?" she said, sinking deeper into her act. "Motherfucker, you think money grows on trees? Huh? If told ya once, I told you a thousand times, ta be good. But no . . . you can't even do dat? . . . You gonna get it now! You be askin' for it! Dyin' fa me ta whip dat ass . . . right, Marvin? Right?"

"Yes," he said bashfully.

"What did you say?" she yelled. "I can't hear you? Did you say somethin'?"

"I said, yes, ma'am. That's what I said," he replied meekly.

"Get ya fat nasty ass across dat bed!" she commanded. "I'ma 'bout ta learn you sumthin'. You li'l bad son of a bitch . . . Ya ass iz grass!"

In a weird way, Tender loved the actual beating. She thought she was striking a blow for the entire black race. She was repaying the man for four hundred years of slavery. The temporary power she had over him made her feel good.

She brought the cat-o'-nine-tails across his back with such force, Marvin screamed like a woman. Even though he had a sock in his mouth, his muffled scream could still be faintly heard.

He was a masochist, loving every minute of it. Accommodating him, Tender brought her whip down again and again until she drew blood. Then it was time to stop. One time she had beaten him so badly, he passed out. She thought she killed him. She carefully wiped down everything in the hotel room she might have touched. She tried to rid the "crime scene" of evidence, her fingerprints. She was never so happy to see a white face in her life the next time he walked in the club. From then on she knew his limits; she knew his threshold for pain. She was careful not to exceed that.

Her next date was also beyond kinky. He too was downright sickening. "Ummm . . . these smell adorable. I love da scent of ya pussy," the Hispanic man said.

Once a month, she had specific instructions to bring him a pair of panties that she had worn during her menstrual cycle. He paid handsomely for her worst drawers. It wasn't the actual undergarment he wanted, he got off on seeing, tasting and smelling her discharge.

More power to the sick bastard, she thought. As long as he kept paying, she would feed his perverted habit.

Another man, a black guy, wanted her to watch him as he masturbated. She wasn't required to touch him, undress or perform any sexual act with him. The only thing he needed was her presence. Most of the times, he couldn't even achieve an erection. On those days, all she had to do was talk dirty to him. Since she charged by the hour, Tender always made sure she had a lot of vulgar sexual things to say. She was becoming as nasty as her clientele wanted her to be. She did everything short of defecating on people.

In addition to her freaky clients, Tender also had men who just wanted to talk. Some would come to the strip club looking to take their minds off certain things or to escape their turbulent world. They simply needed a sympathetic ear or maybe just a female's point of view on the problems they were having with a wife or girlfriend. She would sit and listen, then give them good advice. She would counsel them on their troubles, making them feel good. For the short period of time that they were there, their minds were completely taken off of whatever was worrying them. Gratefully, they would be more than happy to dig into their pockets and give her their hard-earned cash. They compensated her well as a small token of their gratitude.

# CHAPTER
# 15

K AT SANK HER CLAWS into Q and refused to let him go. He was her prized client now. "Q!" she called out, as they lay in bed at his condo. "I'm not good at sharin'! Nigga, you gone havta cut Tender's ass da fuck off."

He had heard this all before from Kat. She was making a habit of stressing him about this bullshit. He didn't like being placed in a position where he was forced to choose. Q was the man. He called the shots and he wanted to see whom he damn well pleased. To him, they all were hos. Quietly, he still liked Tender. It was no secret; he was still testing her water and still giving her money.

Kat had begun to take him personally, claiming him for herself. She began catching feelings from out of nowhere. To him, their relationship was strictly a sex thing, no more, no less. His baby's mother made life a living hell for any female who got too close to him anyway. She ran countless beautiful women out of his life. They were unable to deal with her zany antics. She was a fatal-attraction type of female who never understood it was over between them. To her, it was just as if they were married till death do them part. She was his. Of course, Q led her on, sending her mixed signals by continuing to sleep with her every so often.

Q never succeeded in his ongoing attempts to make her miserable, to run her away. She tolerated his cheating heart, rationalizing to herself that she shared a bond with him that no other woman in the world could claim. They had a child together. His failure to break off their on-again, off-again relationship was something that he would later regret.

"Listen man, would you stop talkin' 'bout dat?" he asked, in between puffs of his blunt. "Goddamn, what dat girl eva do ta you? . . . She don't eva even mention ya name when she 'round me. But you always hatin' on her. . . . You gotta lotta hate in ya blood. Na'mean?"

"Call it whatcha want," she announced. "But you don't know dis bitch like I know dis bitch. Jus' 'cause you fuckin' her, don't make her no angel. . . . Dat ho got mo' shit wit her than a li'l bit . . . don't think she don't. . . . She feel sum type a way 'bout us. You think dat bitch ain't mad cause you chose me? . . . Puhleezze!!! . . . Dat bitch iz swoll . . . shit comin' missin 'round da house all of a sudden . . . and here you iz defendin' da ho! . . . I hope you gotta place fa ha nasty ass ta stay, cause I'ma 'bout to get rid a her ass . . ."

"Dig, I ain't know it was all like dat," he stated. "But could you please do me a favor? And leave me outta it . . . gotta nuff drama dealin' wit my baby's momma. . . . Sound like it don't got nuttin' ta do wit me. . . . Dat shit wuz in da makin' long befo' I came along. . . ."

"Whut you mean, it got nuttin' ta do wit you? Dis got e'rything ta do wit you!" she said maliciously. "If you tell da bitch you don't wanna be bothered, then it's dead, till then it's always gonna be sumthin'."

"I'm not even involvin' myself in dat shit," he told her. "Dat's some young girl shit!!! When I wuz a young boy, gotta kick outta dat. . . . Now dat I'm older I did away wit dat childish shit. . . . Dig? Whut I look like???"

"Okay, I'ma do it!" she spat heatedly. "Since you won't tell her, I'ma tell her! Since you care so much 'bout da bitch's funky feelin'. And if she buck . . . it's gonna be sumthin'. . . . We'll see how much you like her afta I pound her da fuck out!!! We'll see whatcha gonna say then. . . ."

"*Whateva!* . . ." he replied nonchalantly. "Since ya lips iz steady yappin' . . . why don't you put 'em da good use? Gimme some head."

His wish was Kat's command.

OUT OF THE BLUE, Tender received a phone call from Q. It kind of surprised her because they hadn't been seeing much of each other lately. She had backed up off him. She was handling her business, leaving him to handle his. She wasn't going to force herself upon anyone. The day any man didn't want her was the day she didn't want him. One of the worse things in the world is a person caught up in a one-sided relationship.

"Dig," he announced into the receiver, "dis me, Q. In case you don't know who it is?"

"You didn't hafta tell me. I already caught ya voice. . . . It ain't been dat long. You ain't no stranger," she said, without a hint of animosity.

"Dat's good, Tender. You know I stil dig ya ghost," he said cheerfully. "Listen, anyway . . . I ain't call ya ta trouble you or nuttin', and dis ain't no booty call. I miss you. Despite everything, you good peoples, fa sure."

Pausing briefly, Q let his last statement sink in. "Look, I ain't tryin' ta start nuttin'. Or play both sides ta da middle. I got betta things ta do. I ain't on it like dat! I don't even rock like dat.

But dig, ya gurl Kat iz hatin' on you somethin' terrible, fa real. Somethin' terrible. I don't know what you done did ta her. Or she ta you. But da shit don't sound right. Soma da things she said 'bout you don't even match ya character. I had ta check da broad. I'm like whoa, dat ain't got nuttin' ta do wit— You know she copped an attitude? But listen though, word ta da wise. Jus' watch yaself. Get up outta dat house. She ain't got no love fa you. Dat's some real shit right there too . . . na'mean?"

It's like that? Tender thought. Kat was running her mouth to Q about her. At least that's the way she took everything into account.

"Thanks fa lettin' me know," she said. "I know you didn't hafta do dat. But you did."

"Anytime," he responded. "Even if we don't rock like dat no more. We still always gonna be fly, gurl, cause dat's how I do . . . I neva jus' sever my ties. I try ta keep all lines of communication open. Tender, gotta go. Holla at me if you need somethin'. Da boy always got love fa you. We bigger than dat . . . take care. . . ."

"You too, Q. You too," she said, putting an end to their brief conversation. "I will holla atcha if I need somethin'."

KAT AND TENDER BARELY SAW EACH OTHER. When Tender was out, she was in and vice versa. Kat knew where she was at, if she really wanted to find her. All she had to was come to the club. Tender still would leave large sums of money on the kitchen table along with a yellow sticky stationary note that simply read, "For Goldie." She wasn't going to let anyone or anything make her break her promise.

Tender decided to fight fire with fire. She wasn't a coward. To every stripper she knew who knew Kat, even those who didn't, she told them just how Kat really was—really gettin' down. She was an egotistical, self-centered, backbiting, two-faced yellow bitch.

One day, while home alone, she went to take a shower and there was the phone. She hadn't seen the house phone in a minute. Kat had spitefully taken the cordless phone out the kitchen and locked the other in her bedroom. Tender was amazed by her pettiness. Like that hurt her. After all, she had her own cell phone.

As she undressed and was about to enter the shower, the phone rang. She answered it.

"Hello?" She spoke softly into the phone.

"Bitch," a female voice barked, "don't fuckin' try ta be nice ta me . . . not afta you wuz talkin' all dat tough shit da other day."

Tender's eyebrow rose, curiously. This chick must have mistaken her for Kat. She didn't know who this was.

"Excuse me," Tender stated, "I don't even know who dis iz."

"Bitch, don't play dumb wit me. You know who da fuck dis iz," she replied furiously, with venom dripping from her voice. "Dis Q baby momma! Niecey!!! You fuckin' home wrecker. Didn't I tell you ta leave my man alone? Bitch, you hardheaded, huh? I see you gonna really make me hurt you."

Tender thought, Things must be pretty heated, if Q's baby's mother was calling the house, making terroristic threats. She quickly wondered how she got this number. Then she remembered how nosy and resourceful women could be. Especially if they thought their man was cheating. They would violate everything that they stood for. Stopping at nothing till they found out what they needed to know. They weren't below taking a number that appeared too many times on their man's pager or cell phone. Getting a copy of his phone bill or checking his phone while he was fast asleep. They were going to get it one way or another. At least an observant woman would.

A devilish thought crossed Tender's mind at that very moment. Since this chick think I'm Kat, I'll let her believe it. She even instigated their spat, further agitating the woman.

"Bitch, fuck you! You ain't doin' shit ta me! . . . If you wuz fuckin' ya man right he wouldn't be over here fuckin' wit me! Eatin' my pussy . . . aha bitch! Now, what?! How my pussy taste?" Tender yelled into the phone before slamming down the receiver.

After having a good laugh at Kat's expense, she patted herself on the back for that. Clearly she wasn't the same person who joined the ranks of a secret society known as strippers. Her experiences had hardened her soul worse than any callus. She'd always said she wasn't afraid of Kat. Soon she would get her chance to prove it.

But what she didn't know, what she never got a chance to hear, was the irate young lady's vow to kill Kat.

# 16

**G**OLDIE WAS RESTLESS. She hadn't had a peaceful night's sleep since God knows when. The stress of the past few months was manifesting itself on her face, in the form of dark bags under her eyes. She was fired from Sue's Rendezvous strip club after she passed out while on the job. The Ecstasy pills she'd taken had dehydrated her.

She was desperate for money again. She was just about down to her last dollar. She called Kat again but all she had to say was, "Why don't you call my peoples? They'll help you out now."

"Where's Tender? She ain't around? She can't send it?" Goldie asked.

"I don't know how many times I gotta tell you. Tender don't fuck wit us like dat. Dat nigga, Q, got her nose wide open. . . . She's too busy livin' it up. I ain't seen her in weeks. Please."

Goldie thought, First Tender reneged on their agreement to leave. Now she ain't nowhere to be found, especially now that she needed her help so desperately. Some friend she was. In her eyes Tender was worse than Kat.

"Okay, I'ma call 'em taday . . ." Goldie assured her.

"Why don't you do that? They right there, they can help quicker than I could," Kat said.

"You sure you gonna be able to do dat tomorrow?" Goldie asked, referring to the money she had asked Kat to send.

"Yeah!" Kat exploded. "I'ma do my part. You just need ta get off da phone wit me and handle dat. Da gurl's name iz Nikko. I already told her you family . . . so you in . . . aiight? Bye!"

"Hold up a minute," Goldie tried to say, but the line went dead.

Goldie reluctantly dialed the phone number from a pay phone. On the first ring someone answered.

"Helllloooo, Nikko? Dis Kat's friend, Goldie. She told me ta call you. She said you'd be expecting my call."

"Okay, yeah, she did mention you. What took ya so long ta call? You wuz suppose ta holla at me."

"Ummm . . ." she began. "I got caught up."

"Yeah, I feel you," Nikko replied. "But what'z poppin'? What'z really good wit you?"

"Right now, I a li'l fucked up. Had ta leave da club I wuz dancin' at . . . too much drama. . . . My money a li'l funny right now. I need ta start back dancin' but I don't know where no otha clubs at," Goldie told her.

"Where ya rest at?" Nikko asked.

"I'm all da way up in Mount V," she replied quickly.

"Yeah, you up there near west bubba fuck. . . . Dat's da boonies ta me. I stay in Harlem World. So whut you tryin' ta do? You wanna make some money or whut?"

"Yeah, I wanna make some money," Goldie repeated. "Whatcha got in mind? You got somethin' fa me?"

"Umm, I don't know if you ever heard of dis? But tonight they havin' dis shit called Da Brainfest. It's in da Bronx. . . ." Nikko said.

"Na, I neva heard a dat. Whut iz it?" she asked.

"It's jus' a big event dat some promoters are throwin'. They bringin' in a lotta strippers and niggas . . . and people jus' be gettin' their fuck and suck on," Nikko explained. "It's mad money ta be made . . . I'm sayin' it's da move. I can put you down, if you want to."

This wasn't exactly what Goldie had in mind, but she didn't have much of a choice. The rent was due soon and she had to feed her ever present drug habit. So with the prospect of doing both, she agreed to participate in this sex fest.

"Aiight, I'm down . . ." she said, accepting the offer. "But how am I gonna get there?"

"How fast can you be ready? You got somethin' ta wear, right?"

"Yeah, I gotta few outfits. I could be ready inna few minutes," she explained.

"Good. Tell me exactly where ya live and I'll be up there inna half an hour ta getcha," Nikko responded.

"You know where da last stop on the two train iz? . . . Well, I live not too far from there. I live on Third Street."

THE FLYERS FOR THE BRAINFEST had been circling around for months. They had been passed out in barbershops, gambling spots, private parties and strip clubs throughout the city. It was a highly anticipated event. Everybody knew that everything goes at the Brainfest. There would be literally dozens upon dozens of naked and partially clothed strippers in attendance, and even more paying customers.

At one time this event was strictly a backdoor, hush-hush word-of-mouth type of thing. But with the success of each event, the promoters grew more confident and bolder. They had a hot product on their hands. Guys came from near and far to witness and partake in it. Tickets for the event were twenty dollars, and even more at the door. The flyers said the event would be held at one place, only to be moved at the last minute to another secret location, to avoid being busted by the police.

When Nikko finally arrived to pick up Goldie, she realized that Nikko bore a striking resemblance to Kat. She was just a shade darker and a few inches shorter. Otherwise they could have passed for sisters.

They arrived at the secret location, a popular Bronx basketball gym, just as the crowds of men began to file in. Security was tight. Everyone entering, with the exception of the strippers, was thoroughly searched, patted down for weapons. Anything was liable to happen here.

The gym was dimly lit with a makeshift stage, just off to the right of the center of the floor. Tender and Nikko used the locker rooms to change. After securing their knapsacks in a locker, they took to the floor.

"Whut'z up, shorty? . . . How much fa sum head?" one dude asked.

"Lemme hit dat mommy!" someone else said. "Dat ass lookin' kinda fat!" "I'll break ya muthafuckin' back!!" "You can't handle dis dick." "I ain't no joke . . . fa real. . . ."

"*Da muy baseo, Mommy*! (Gimme a kiss, Mommy)" yet another man spoke in Spanish, taking the liberty to fondle her buttocks as she passed.

It seemed like every time she looked up, someone different was in her face propositioning her. There were strippers of different shapes and sizes everywhere, along the walls, up in the bleachers, on stage, walking through the thick crowds of men, doing their thing. She saw guys engaging in oral sex in front of everyone. Strippers were lap dancing, wall dancing, jerking guys off, and committing every imaginable sexual act known to man.

On stage, one stripper had lots of guys' attention; she was putting on a show, using two glow-in-the-dark dildos. She rammed them into every opening. It seemed as if she was enjoying it just as much as they were. They swarmed on her, like rats to cheese, savagely pawing at her private parts.

This was a modern day Sodom and Gomorrah, the biblical city that God had destroyed with fire and brimstone—because the people were committing such sexually deviant and perverse acts. Goldie hadn't ever seen anything like it, not on this scale. The gym was packed with freaks on both sides of the coin.

It didn't take long for Goldie to get into the swing of things. She began taking dates back to the secure VIP area, servicing their sexual needs. Back and forth she went—each time she brought someone different. In the back of her mind she was counting up all the money she made. Immediately after this, she planned on going to see one of the drug boys around her way. She was going to get high, high, high.

As the weeks went on, when Goldie wasn't doing private parties, she stripped at sleazy clubs in The Bronx. She bounced around The Golden Lady, The Wedge and Harry's Triangle in the Hunt's Point section, from one club to another. Nikko introduced her to these places and took the majority of Goldie's pay. She left her just enough money to pay her weekly room rent, carfare and her habit.

Alone in her room she would get high and write in her diary. On days like these, her mother's ghost would come out and haunt her. Different images flashed through her mind. Her memory hung over Goldie like an ominous black cloud.

She prayed, read and studied the word of God, searching for some meaning in life. But as hard as she tried to put her life in perspective, she couldn't.

Nikko picked Goldie up, supposedly to take her to work. "Where we goin'?" she questioned. "Da club ain't dis way."

"Would you shut up fa a minute? Be da fuck easy," Nikko cursed. "Listen, we ain't fuckin' wit dat club shit no mo'. I got a betta way fa you ta make some easy money. I know dis guy who takes pictures . . . naked pictures of women. He always lookin' fa fresh faces, so I figured I'd take you down there and let you get dat money. . . ."

Just like Kat, Nikko was bossy. She wasn't askin' Goldie, she was tellin' her. Half of the time, Goldie didn't know if she was coming or going. Nikko had begun to feed Goldie drugs.

"Here take these," Nikko said, as she passed her a few Ecstasy pills. Kat had told Nikko just how to control Goldie. "It'll make you feel good. . . . Don't you wanna feel good? . . ."

Without a second thought, she snatched the drugs out her hand and gobbled them down. This was all she needed to get by.

The photo session that Nikko had promised turned out to be on the set of a porno movie. Goldie was to be the star of the show. Everyone on the set knew what to expect but Goldie. Drugged up, she performed like a champ. She did as she was told.

Every day she was inching closer and closer toward death. She was finding it increasingly more difficult to hold on. She was bouncing between porn film studios and her room where she got high and read the Bible. She stumbled across a startling revelation, in Ecclesiastes. She read out loud.

> . . . *Everything has its Time. To everything there is a season.*
> *A time for every purpose under the heavens . . . a time to*
> *weep. And a time to laugh . . . a time to gain. And a time to*
> *lose . . . a time to keep silent. And a time to Die. . . .*

Those words hit her like a ton of bricks. There it was right there in the Bible, a time to die. It was her time to die. She had made up her mind not to fight it any longer. Goldie imagined that it wouldn't be long before the police kicked down her door and arrested her.

"Now, I lay me down to sleep." She recited a prayer. "I pray the Lord my soul to keep. And if I should die before I wake, I pray the Lord my soul to take."

Getting up off her knees, she went to her nightstand and grabbed a bottle of pills. Dumping them in her hand, she cupped the contents of the bottle in her hands and threw them in her mouth. She tilted her head back and reached for a glass of water to wash them down. She swallowed them down. She wrote a note asking that her diary be forwarded to Kat's home address. She hoped it would find its way to Tender's hands.

# 17

I GOTTA PACKAGE for Tonya Morris?" the UPS delivery man stated, as Tender opened the door. "Miss, are you Tonya Morris? . . ."

Tender shot him a peculiar look before answering. She hadn't heard her real name called in a while. "Yeah, dat's me . . . What iz dis? . . . I ain't order nuttin' . . ."

"I just deliver it. I didn't send it," he remarked sarcastically. "The name's on the box . . . Now, would you sign right here for me."

Tender grabbed what appeared to be, to her, an electronic clipboard, and scribbled her name in the designated area. Then the man handed her a small, rectangular, plain brown box. It looked like a book. Tender closed the door and opened the box. She was curious to see who the package was from and what was inside.

The owner of the rooming house had discovered Goldie's body, along with a suicide note, when she came to collect her weekly rent.

The homicide unit had been called to the scene of the crime. They found no signs of foul play. The county medical examiner established the cause of death as suicide. Goldie's body sat unclaimed in the morgue for a few days before she was buried in a Potter's Field. Her final resting place was among the nameless and faceless society, the homeless.

A chill slithered up Tender's spine. Sitting on her bed, she opened up the diary. As she began to read, the pages seemed to come to life. In her mind she could hear Goldie's voice narrating the events of her life.

> *. . . I don't believe I jus kilt my mother??? . . . I didn't mean to. It wuz a accident I swear ta God . . . Musta accidentally hit da stove and turned on the gas runnin' tryin ta get away from her . . . She wuz beatin' da hell out of me . . . Jus wanted ta get away . . . Ta let her cool off . . . I neva seen her like dis before. And all cause of Angel. She found one a his old letters he had written me from jail. I knew I shoulda ripped 'em up and thrown 'em away. But I jus like readin' 'em over and over again . . . I'm so stupid! If only I had . . . listened ta her. None a dis would neva have happened . . .*

This was the first entry in the diary, the date had not been recorded. Her writing was messy and bunched together, the letters sometimes went over the boundaries of the line.

Tender skipped through the pages.

> *. . . Angel jus finished beatin' da shit out of me. Fa nuttin'. Some boy stopped me and asked me fa directions . . . and he thought the boy wuz hollerin' at me . . . But he wuzn't . . . He's so damn jealous . . . He jus like his father . . . A cheater and a woman beater . . . Dis time he went too far . . . I been bleedin' fa da past hour . . . think I lost da baby . . . I'm too*

*scared ta go ta da hospital . . . Wish I woulda listened ta*
*mom . . . she told me he wuz no good . . .*

The average teenage happenings were noticeably absent. There
was no girly gossip or talk of school, friends and family. There was
no joy, enthusiasm in her words, only sadness and grief. With
each entry came more misery and suffering. Reading the diary
was like watching a movie of Goldie's life. She could see and feel
her pain. Goldie had successfully documented her sorrow. Overcome by emotion, Tender wiped away a tear. She thought she
had a rough life; it was nothing compared to Goldie's.

*. . . livin' on da street iz tougher than I thought . . . but it still*
*beats livin' wit Angel . . . ain't gotta worry 'bout him kickin'*
*my azz no more . . . i ran into dis girl from hiz buildin' she*
*told me he got locked up . . . wit all these guns . . . da police*
*ran up in one a his dope houses and caught him . . . dat's*
*good fa him . . . you reap what you sow . . .*

*. . . last nite met dis girl name Kat in center city . . . it's crazy*
*how we met . . . she offered me a place ta stay . . . couldn't*
*believe dat? . . . i went too! . . . i ain't crazy . . . her house iz*
*da bomb . . . she gave me my own room . . . haven't had dat*
*since . . . since . . . a long time ago . . . she's real nice . . . she*
*promised ta take me down ta her job . . . and get me one . . .*
*dag, she neva said where she works . . . dat's funny? . . .*
*maybe i didn't catch it? . . . o' well . . . can't wait till*
*tomorrow . . .*

*. . . some job she got . . . can't believe she's a stripper . . .*
*shoulda neva told her my bizness . . . 'bout my mother . . .*
*she used it against me . . . she forced me ta strip . . . once*
*again i'm fucked . . . i got nowhere ta go . . . Remind me*

*neva ta open my big mouf again . . . can't trust no one . . .*
*sorry, only you . . .*

*i'ma slave . . . Kat ain't nuttin' but a pimp . . . got me fuckin'*
*all kinda nigga's . . . she call it datin' . . . it ain't like no date i*
*eva hearda . . . she be takin' all my money . . . she got me*
*ona allowance . . . boy, wuz i eva wrong 'bout her . . . dis*
*bitch iz mean and wicked . . . all she do iz threaten me . . .*
*i'm scareda her . . .*

*'it's new year's day . . . so whut . . . big deal . . . las year wuz*
*da worst year of my life . . . you aready know why . . . i*
*doubt if dis year be any different . . . i gotta get outta here*
*. . . i can't take no mo' . . . seem like dis bitch Kat gettin'*
*worster by da day . . . she think she da shit . . . dat bitch . . .*

*. . . tanite i got jumped at da club cause of Kat . . . they really*
*wanted her . . . but dat bitch just dropped me off and kept*
*goin' 'bout her bizness . . . i always new her mouf wuz gonna*
*get us in trouble . . .*

*. . . i tried exstacy fa da first time . . . Kat gave it ta me . . .*
*she didn't tell whut it was till afta . . . Dat shit made me feel*
*good . . . i up in da club dancin' my azz off . . . i like dat shit*
*. . . it's da best thing Kat eva did fa me. . . .*

As Tender read, her anger grew. Rage bubbled inside her. She couldn't believe that Kat got Goldie hooked on drugs. It was just another way of keeping her in line. Things were getting stranger by the minute.

*. . . Kat found anotha stray kitten . . . Her name Tonya but*
*we renamed her Tender . . . hope she don't do her dirty too*

*. . . yeah, right who am i kiddin'? . . . it's in her nature . . .
anyway da girl seemed ta be nice . . . Can't get too close ta
her though . . . member what happened last time i thought
somebody wuz my friend . . . gotta figure out a way ta tell
her . . . what da real deal iz . . . can't let it go down like dat
again . . .*

*. . . woke up last nite ina cold sweat . . . keep havin' these
bad dreams . . . they won't go away . . . it's bad enuff i gotta
live with what i did . . . now i gotta sleep wit it too . . . When
iz it gonna stop???*

Tender scanned through a few pages. From what she could see it
was more of the same. Reading it was depressing; she couldn't
imagine how Goldie was actually feeling at the time.

*. . . i'm in N.Y.C. now . . . on da run cause da police r lookin'
fa me. . . . Don't really like it here . . . but what choice do i
hav . . . either dis or jail . . . Livin' in sum roomin' house in
Mt. Vernon . . . seem like sumthin' bad always happenin' ta
me . . . why? . . . dat shit ain't fair . . .*

*. . . tried ta call Tender taday . . . Kat picked up . . . said
Tender don't fuck wit me like dat no more!! . . . can't believe
she turned her back on me like dat . . . i know ima deadman
now!!! . . . Kat ain't gonna do nuttin' fa me . . . She wuz my
only hope . . .*

*. . . been gettin' high as a muthafucka lately . . . gotta admit
i'm addicted . . . i luv da way xstacy makes me feel . . . even
though it jus cost me my job at a club . . . i'm slippin' . . .
passed out in da club . . . fuck it . . .*

• • •

*i'm out here on E . . . don't know how i'ma pay dis weeks rent . . . spoke ta Kat again. she said Tender fuckin' wit Q real heavy . . . and ain't got no time fa nuttin' else . . . she said she wuz gonna send me some loot . . . western union . . . don't really like ta depend on her . . . but whut can i do??? . . . finally called Kat'z peepz . . . Nikko . . . she pose ta cum up here and take me ta dis strip club in da Bronx. . . .*

*. . . Nikko jus as bad as Kat . . . dem bitches sorta look alike too . . . she be puttin' pressure on me 'bout da paper i'm makin' . . . here we go again . . .*

*. . . been readin' da bible alot lately . . . and gettin' high . . . dat's all i been doin' . . . besides strippin' . . . been goin' on alota dates too . . . Nikko puttin' me up to it . . . Can't believe what i just did??? i filmed a porno movie . . . my mother must be turnin' over ina grave right now . . . can't believe it . . . gettin' tireda livin' like dis . . . dis ain't a life fa nobody . . . i'm ready ta go . . . ready ta die. . . .*

The last entry was a note addressed to Tender.

*if you're readin' these lines then dat means i'm dead & gone. Yeah, i kilt myself, put myself outta my misery . . . Please, Tender don't cry fa me . . . I took my own life. I accept my fate, whateva it maybe. I couldn't go on livin' like dat . . . dat can't be life!!! . . . now, I hope you see what I wuz goin' through . . . I couldn't tell you da things I really felt you should know 'bout me or Kat. My hands were tied behind my back . . . Kat knew too much and she always threw it up in my face . . . but outta all people I neva thought you would turn ya back on me. Why Tender? Thought we wuz fam? U said dat U was gonna help me . . . instead u hurt me more than you'll eva know . . . i wouldna guess u wuz really like dat . . . guess absence don't really make da heart grow fonda afta all . . . wit u it wuz outta sight outta mind . . . they say you neva really know a person till you live wit 'em or get in trouble wit 'em . . . then da real them comes out . . . dat's da God's honest truth . . . u showed ya tru colors when i need u da most . . . a friend in need iz a friend indeed . . . hope u & Q r happy . . . thanks fa nuttin' . . . enjoy ya life!!!*

*4eva ya dog*
*Goldie*

Tender decided not to go to the club today for two reasons. One was out of respect to Goldie. The other was to lay in wait on Kat. She had to come home sooner or later. And when she did, Tender planned on being right there waiting. It was time they had a little talk.

# 18

K AT ARRIVED AT THE HOUSE later that night, fresh off a sexual romp with Q. She had all but abandoned the strip scene. She didn't have to strip. What for? Now she had Q taking care of her. And if that wasn't enough, she also had Tender handing over her money to her too, thinking that it was going toward Goldie's lawyer fees. Yeah, right. Imagine that, she thought. That was a good one.

Sticking her key in the lock, she unlocked the door and crossed the threshold. Thoughts of money ran through her mind as she walked down the hallway. She hadn't expected to see Tender sitting there at the kitchen table. Her presence startled her.

"Well, look whut da cat drug in? . . ." Kat said sarcastically. "Whut bringz you here dis time a nite? Ain't you suppose ta be at da club? Or somethin'?? . . ."

Tender shot her a no-nonsense look. She cut straight to the chase.

"Goldie's dead!!! . . ." she announced. "She's dead!!! . . . She killed herself!!! . . ."

Kat looked to see if she was joking or not. Kat was trying to be fly about it. But she was pacing backward and forth. "So whut you want me ta do? . . . Cry? She did it ta herself . . . How stupid could she be?? . . . She wuz a li'l troublemaker anyway . . . dat's good fa her!!! . . . I don't feel da least bit sorry fa her . . . Maybe now da fuckin' cops will leave me da fuck alone? . . . She made my whole house hot as shit anyway. Cops comin' here lookin' fa her and shit. The bitch was crazy and weak-minded."

"Kat, you must be outta ya fuckin' mind! . . ." she cursed loudly. ". . . How da fuck could you even fix ya face ta even say sum shit like dat??? . . . Huh? . . . You just as much responsible fa her death as she iz. She shot Jules fa you! It wuzn't her or my beef. Dat wuz ya beef! Who started all dat drama with Cookie. You! Not nobody else . . . so let's not get dis shit twisted. . . ."

The contours of Kat's face changed immediately. Her mouth drew back tightly to her teeth. She squinted her eyes. She couldn't believe Tender had the audacity to stand up to her. After all, she was the boss. She was in charge. She ran things around here. Kat was used to going unchallenged, Bogarting her way through life, she preyed on the weak. She was so used to having her way, doing her thing. Anything she wanted to do, the reality was, who was going to stop her?

"Kat, I know everything! . . . I know dat you wuz pimping Goldie. I know dat you wuz tryin' ta pimp me . . . maybe dat's why you didn't really like Jules? Y'all too much alike . . . y'all afta da same thing . . . I know you turned Goldie out . . . had her hooked on E pills . . . I know 'bout ya so-called peepz in N.Y. . . . Nikko . . . I'm willin' ta bet . . . anything it wuz you who put her up on Goldie . . . you told her ta use Goldie . . . ta take her shit like you wuz doin' . . . huh? . . . And don't think I don't know you been talkin' behind my back . . . Here I am right here!! . . . Say it ta my face . . . Bitch, you bad!!! . . ."

"*Bitch!!!*" Kat yelled as she swung wildly, failing to connect.

". . . wanna piece a me?? . . . I'ma give ya whatcha' lookin' fa!!!
. . . I'ma beat dat ass!!!. . . ."

Tender quickly ducked, easily avoiding the blow. Had it found
its intended target, her face, it might have done some serious
damage. Kat was fighting off pure emotions. That was a dangerous thing. It tended to make a person rush and take unnecessary
risks.

Kat threw her punch so hard, that it spun her almost completely around. Tender capitalized on her mistake by jumping on
her back. They came crashing down on the kitchen floor. Tender
landed on top and sat on Kat's back. She grabbed a handful of
Kat's hair and began ramming her head into the floor.

". . . Yeah, dis fa Goldie . . ." she commented, while banging
her head. ". . . you rotten-ass bitch!! . . . Whatcha' gonna do
now??? Huh??? . . ."

Blood began to gush from Kat's head. She was totally at
Tender's mercy. She did the only thing she could do. She gave up.

"I give . . ." Kat cried. "I give . . . dat's enuff!"

"Huh?? . . . Whatcha' say? . . . I can't hear you? . . ." she
replied, pausing in midair with a handful of Kat's hair. "Excuse
me, you said somethin'? . . ."

"You got it!!! I don't want no more. Ya killin' me . . ." she
pleaded.

"I should kill ya muthafuckin' ass!!! . . . Bitch, I should
kill you!!! . . . Now you know how Goldie felt . . . Now, you
know!!! . . ." Tender ranted.

Tender knew from experience that most times a person with a
big mouth couldn't fight. Tough talk was their only defense. If
you could get past that, then the battle was won. And that was the
case here. Tender took the fight right out of her. When Kat
missed her golden opportunity to sneak Tender, she was
doomed. She planned on stunning her, and staying on top of her.
But it didn't turn out that way. Her plan failed miserably.

"... Where da fuck iz my money??? ... What you do wit all dat money I wuz givin' you?? ... I want my fuckin' money!! ... You hear me??? ... Huh?? ... Answer me!! ... Where's my money??? ...." she demanded to know.

"I got it ... it's in da bank ... I'll give it ta ya tomorrow ..." she promised. "... I promise ... You'll get it tomorrow. ...."

"I betta, bitch!!! ...." she warned. "... I betta get it tomorrow!!! ... E'ry red fuckin' cent betta be there ... Or else I'ma whup ya ass e'ry time I see you ... You hear me?? ... I mean it ... I ain't fuckin' playin' either."

With that said, she released her grip on Kat's hair. She watched her head slowly bang on the floor.

Tender went in her bedroom to gather up her things. This was never her house in no way shape or form. She was just mad it took her so long to see that. "But better late than never," she mused.

"Hav my money tomorrow!!! ...." she reiterated. "... Meet me outside da club wit it ... All of it."

Kat stood in the bathroom mirror, wiping the blood off her face.

Tender left the house, slamming the door behind her, and hopped into a cab. She was headed for a hotel.

WAITING IMPATIENTLY in front of the club, Tender paced back and forth. Where was Kat at? What was taking her so long? Had she double-crossed her? If she had, Tender planned on sitting on her porch till she came home. Then she'd give her another beating, only this time she wouldn't stop.

Looking up, she spotted Kat's white truck pulling up to the curb. It's about time, she thought. The sight of Kat's truck was a big relief. She needed that money. Her days as a stripper were over. She finally decided to leave the game.

"Tender?" she called out passively. "Here, come get ya money."

As soon as she got close to the truck, Kat's passenger doors flew open. Out jumped two heavyset, gruesome-looking girls. Kat had gone back to her old neighborhood and recruited the toughest girls she could find. Since she couldn't beat Tender in a fair fight, she planned on jumping her. Kat was gonna got even by any means neccessary.

"C'mere, bitch!!!" one girl yelled, as she rushed Tender.

Taken by surprise, Tender was overwhelmed, she had no choice but to lock horns with the bigger girl. Meanwhile, Kat quickly exited the truck and joined the ruckus.

"Grab her ass!!" Kat instructed her hired help. "Hold her still!! . . ."

Kat had her right hand wrapped with a rag, to conceal the pair of brass knuckles she wore. She wanted to kill Tender for what she did to her. But Kat feared jail too much to do that. She had a little son to raise, so she figured a beat-down would be good enough.

Raising her fist, she cocked back, throwing a punch as hard as she could. Tender watched helplessly, she was hemmed up in a full nelson, as Kat's fist sailed through the air in slow motion. This time Kat found her target, hitting her dead in the face.

The blow was thrown so hard, both the girls and Tender reeled back on impact. A satisfying smile appeared on Kat's face as she extracted her revenge. Again and again, she pulverized her face. Lumps appeared magically.

"Bitch, you ain't getting' shit!!! . . ." Kat barked. "You musta been crazy if you thought I wuz givin' up dat money . . . You'll have ta kill me ta get it!!! . . ."

Two men exiting the club stumbled upon this one-sided fight. "Hey, what da fuck y'all doin'? . . . Let dat girl go! . . . Why don't you shoot her a fair one?"

Kat and company panicked, releasing the hold on Tender; they jumped in the truck and peeled off. Tender fell to the ground, knocked out cold.

# 19

TENDER WOKE UP IN THE HOSPITAL. How could she be so stupid? she wondered. She made a costly mistake by trusting Kat. That wouldn't happen again.

Tender may have been down, but she wasn't out. Not by a long shot. In fact she had Kat right where she wanted her. It was time to play her trump card.

For a week she laid up in the hospital, for precautionary measures, under observation of her doctors, recuperating. Tender used the time to plot against Kat. She must have gone over her plan a million times in her mind. To her, it was foolproof. All she had to do was put the two pieces in place and things would take of themselves. It was just that simple.

Every dog has its day, Tender thought; and if it were left up to her, Kat's was coming soon. All she had to do was speed things up.

Walking down the hall, Kat went into the phone booth. She opened her flip cell phone, carefully searching its phone book for a specific phone number. Finding it, she punched the numbers into the public pay phone. On the first ring someone picked up.

"... Hey, ho!!" she cursed into the phone. "Dis Kat!! ... Yeah, it's me, bitch ... Listen, I wanted you ta be da first ta know ... Me and Q iz gettin' married soon ... Yeah, bitch, you heard me right!!! ... Married!!! ... I wanna know can his daughter be aparta our weddin'??? ... So, da fuck what? ... It's his child toooo!!! ... Faget it then ... Let me tell ya sumthin' else ... I'm pregnant ... six months ... Eat ya heart out ... You ain't gonna do a muthafuckin' thing ta me! ... Bring ya black ass right down here then ... I live on ... I'll be waitin'. I got somethin' fa ya ass ... C'mon!!! ..."

Tender knew today was Friday, the first of the month. And she also knew that Kat went to pick up her son at school around this time. Faithfully, she went and got him, spending the day with him. She had just hung up the phone after antagonizing Niecey, Q's crazy baby's mother, as if she were Kat. By giving her Kat's home address, she sealed her fate.

Leaving her house, Kat never suspected anything was wrong. She had no reason to. She was looking forward to spending some time with her son. She had been slacking in that department lately. Ever since she hooked up with Q, her son's time had diminished drastically. Today she was going to make it up to him, she was going to buy him those new sneakers he asked for. That oughta make him happy, she thought.

Walking toward her truck, she never paid any mind to the dark tinted windowed Honda Accord that was parked directly behind her car. Just as she was about to enter her truck, the driver's-side door of the car flew open. Gun in hand, Niecey exited her car.

"Kat? ..." Niecey called as she raised the gun.

Kat looked at her with sheer fear in her eyes. "Noooooo!!!!" she begged. "Don't shoot!"

"Take dis, you big mouth bitch!!! . . ." came the reply.

Simultaneously, she fired a shot, from a small .22 caliber handgun, directly into Kat's skull from point-blank range. Kat died instantly. And she never even knew why.

Tender found out about the murder on the news. A sly smile spread across her lips. Somehow she felt good about this evil deed. Good riddance, she thought. The world was now a better place.

"Excuse me, miss, ya face look kinda familiar. . . . Don't I know you from somewhere? . . ."

Busy braiding a client's hair, Tender looked the man directly in the face, to see if she recognized him. She didn't. But it was still a possibility he came in contact with her in her previous life as a stripper. She couldn't be a hundred percent certain.

"Nah, you don't know me . . ." she replied. "I ain't from Philly . . . I'm from York, York, PA . . . Eva heard of it?"

"Yeah, I hearda it. Neva been there though." he answered. "But I swear, I know you from somewhere. . . . I don't neva forget a face. . . ."

Tender turned back around, ignoring the man. She had lots of clients lined up, waiting to get their hair done. She probably would get that kind of response from different men from time to time. If her past occupation did surface, then she would deal with it. She wouldn't deny it, she promised herself. That was in the past. She had done that out of ignorance. Everyone had done something in their lifetime that they weren't so proud of—everyone.

After a year of fast money, false friendship and broken hearts, Tender was walking away from the stripping game. Though she never did get the money to open her own beauty parlor, she was working and saving money up for it. Only now she was going to start her business with clean honest money. She had reason to be optimistic. She was alive, and the future looked bright.

T HE IDEA FOR THIS NOVEL came to me while I was incarcerated. I heard so much about strippers and strip clubs
from the other inmates. Each busload of men brought more stories of strippers. They sparked my curiosity. At the time, I had
never been to or had no desire to go to a strip club. But I promised myself, when I was released, I would make it there.

My first few times in a club, I would lay in the cut and just ob-
serve, getting a feel for this foreign atmosphere. I turned down so
many lap dances and other services, it wasn't funny. I wanted
them to respect me. And I knew from my years in the drug game,
once money exchanges hands, I would be considered a trick. And
every time I entered that particular club, I would be treated like
one. I would be rushed like I was a fiend who came to cop. So if I
gave a stripper some money, it was for nothing. Like here you go
Ma, that's for your pocket. To this day, I never got a lap dance. I'm
not into being teased anyway.

I always thought that these clubs were for only a certain type
of guys—desperate or perverted ones. Boy, was I in for a surprise. I saw regular dudes, just like me. The sight of this sort of
relaxed me and made me feel less out of place. I have to admit,
there were some drop-dead gorgeous women in the clubs,
women with flawless bodies. Then you see others that make you
say, "What the hell is she doing in here? She got some nerve!"

Strippers are some strange creatures. They automatically

turn distrustful whenever conversation with them gets personal. Some of them are so damn fake it's a shame.

The one question that gnawed at my brain was what would make a female do this? How could a female put a price on something so priceless? I was amazed how they pranced around half-naked, damn near naked and sometimes completely naked, in front of complete strangers without a bit of shame. That was one thing I couldn't get over.

I've been incarcerated for numerous years, in different states, in many state facilities, and while incarcerated I was subject to endless strip searches. And each and every time I was ordered to strip, I felt some kinda way about it.